The Lamb

The Lamb

Gina Jobe

RESOURCE *Publications* · Eugene, Oregon

THE LAMB

Resource Publications
An Imprint of Wipf and Stock Publishers
199 W. 8th Ave., Suite 3
Eugene, OR 97401

www.wipfandstock.com

PAPERBACK ISBN: 978-1-7252-7734-2
HARDCOVER ISBN: 978-1-7252-7733-5
EBOOK ISBN: 978-1-7252-7735-9

Manufactured in the U.S.A.   06/18/20

1

"Behold! The Lamb of God who takes away the sin of the world!"

JOHN 1:29 (NKJV)

TEN TINY FINGERTIPS TURNED white as their grip tightened. Legs strained on tiptoes to hold the small form as tall as possible. Big brown eyes peered over the top of the crude corral, growing wider and wider at the sight before them.

Suddenly, the dark eyes blinked, and the small form turned to take off across the rocky, brush spattered ground toward the mudbrick dwelling a few hundred feet away.

"Hannah! Hannah! I saw it! Come quick! Micah told me to come and get you if anything happened!"

A surprised face peaked out from behind a weaving loom to see the tousled haired boy with wide eyes and frantically waving arms who had appeared so suddenly in the courtyard.

"Slow down Nathaniel. Now catch your breath and begin again, slowly." The dancing eyes and slight upward curve of the mouth betrayed the amusement and love of the admonisher.

Nathaniel swallowed hard as he took a deep breath and began again. "It's the mama sheep! She's having her baby . . . right now! I saw the head start to come out! It was in a slimy, red sac and . . ."

"All right, all right. I'm coming. There's no need to go into the gruesome details." The older sibling wrinkled her nose in disgust as she set a shuttle of spun wool down on the wooden stool and gracefully lifted her tall, slender form to follow her little brother to the object of his excited interest. Not wasting a moment, Nathaniel grabbed the outstretched hand and took off once more across the clearing, dragging his laughing sister behind him.

When they arrived at the sheepfold, a bit disheveled and out of breath, the sight that awaited them was, indeed, worthy of the little boy's enthusiasm. There, in a patch of dry, thirsty grass, lay a mother sheep breathing heavily as a tiny wet head and two front legs protruded from her lower abdomen.

The two observers stood in silent reverence as the mother struggled to expel the tiny offspring from her bulging body, lifting her back end slightly with every push. They watched as she rose to her feet, still pushing, slimy strands of mucus hanging loosely off the little nose and hooves of the exiting offspring. Nathaniel had been accurate in his description of the rather messy process.

Hannah drew a deep breath. As many times as she had witnessed birth in her fifteen years, it had never ceased to rouse a sense of wonder from deep within her. Here she was witnessing a part of the amazing concept called creation; something that did not exist a few months ago was now living and breathing and, at this moment, intensely attempting to remove itself from its mother.

As she stood there, Hannah wondered what it had been like for Eve to experience the very first of this great miracle. Did she wonder why her belly was swelling? What a curious thing it must have been to first lay eyes on the tiny, wriggling, helpless bit of humanity that had sprung forth out of her own body. To experience the joys and sorrows of motherhood with no previous example to follow must have been both a challenge and a wonder, to behold the small disproportionate body sprouting, a bit clumsily at times, into the strong figure of a man, to listen as the first garbled attempts at communication evolved into decipherable words and phrases, to watch with wonder as the totally dependent developed slowly into the independent . . .

"Do you think it will be ok?" The soft, serious little voice broke into her thoughts.

By this time the lamb had dropped out onto the ground and was lying very still as the mother sheep nudged it with her muzzle and began licking its face. After a moment, the tiny ears flicked.

"It looks like it." Hannah put a hand on the boy's shoulder, gaze still locked on the now wriggling little bundle of wet wool.

"The little guy is fine," a deeper voice cut in. "You did good, Nathaniel."

Nathaniel turned, beaming as he basked in the compliment of his big brother who was walking towards them pulling a wagonload of leaves and wild vines.

Hannah turned, glancing down at the wagon and then back up, questioningly.

Micah shrugged. "There just isn't enough grass left for them in the fields, not even far out from the village. They are looking so lean, and with the extra ones to feed and now a nursing ewe . . ."

"But Samuel will be back soon to get his sheep," Nathaniel cut in looking from one face to the other.

Hannah and Micah exchanged glances, and a sadness crept into Hannah's eyes as she turned her face quickly back to the newborn lamb. The expression did not go unnoticed by the boy. He tugged at his sister's arm. "Hannah? Samuel will be back, right?"

Hannah swiped at her eyes, took a deep breath, and turned back to Nathaniel. "Of course, he will. Now, what are you going to call the little lamb?"

The concerned look vanished from the boy's face as the thought of naming the baby sheep wiped all other thoughts from his mind. "Really? I can name him?"

Micah reached out and tousled the curly mop atop the boy's head. "Well, it seems only fitting that the one who watched him take his first look around this world should give him a name."

Nathaniel straightened his shoulders and raised his chin, bearing the huge responsibility with pride. The serious little face showed such intensity of thought that Hannah had to turn her head and cough to hide a laugh.

After a moment or two of brow wrinkled thought, the boy solemnly declared, "His name will be Shalom."[1]

~

As she watched him walk away, her stomach turned with revulsion. The contempt she felt for the parting form could be matched only by that which she felt for her own wretched existence.

Athalia turned her head quickly, fearing that she might be sick. She sat down and leaned her head back against a stone pillar, closing her eyes to block out the magnificent temple enclosing her with all its hideous beauty. This place had been her abode for as long as she could remember, and soon, she feared, it would house yet another unsuspecting and completely helpless victim. Her hand rose to rest protectively on her belly.

Her thoughts flitted to the one whose body had been home to her own developing one fifteen years before. Behind closed eyelids Athalia could see the face clearly, but it was the eyes to which Athalia's mind clung. They were eyes that held Athalia in their warmth and love and delight. They were eyes that understood her and accepted her. They were eyes that knew all, and yet forgave all. They were eyes that smiled.

Athalia opened her own tired eyes and sighed. What was the use? In truth, Athalia had no knowledge whatsoever of the woman who had given her life. She had been told only that as an infant she had been abandoned on the steps of this very temple where she had been found by one of the priests: A gift to the gods? A disappointed father who had wanted a son? Plausible explanations. Certainly, neither was unheard of here in Samaria.

Athalia fingered the tiny wooden flute by her side. It and she were all that the woven basket had held that day.

A piercing feminine laugh pulled her from her thoughts. She glanced out to the courtyard from which she had just come. The natural beauty of it seemed disgustingly dichotomous to the ugly, wretched acts that were performed there daily.

---

1. *Shalom* is a Hebrew word meaning *peace* or *wellness*

The distinctive laugh, which could belong to no other than Asdrubal, once again rang out indicating that the ritual act was undoubtedly being performed with some man who had chosen this day to pay tribute to Baal. How Asdrubal could manage to appear always so thrilled to perform Athalia had never been able to figure out. "It's my name," she had told Athalia once when she had inquired. "Asdrubal means Baal is my helper. When I get to feeling like I will positively scream if another coin is tossed my way, I just close my eyes and remember that Baal is my helper. It is for him that I perform, and I will do it gladly."

Athalia's gaze rose to the engraving on the pillar against which she rested. Chiseled into the stone was Baal, that vile deity who gave excuse to all who did what they pleased with her body. There he was with the head of a bull, seated on a throne with a club in one hand and a thunderbolt in the other, the master of the weather which played such a vital part in the prosperity of Samaria.

Athalia's lips tightened. She glared at the bas-relief as if, by her hate-filled stare, she could force him to look away in intimidation. For Athalia did not fear Baal as did the others who dwelt in the temple.

She had not always carried such animosity towards the deity. When she was younger Athalia had been taught to fear and revere Baal, and she had obeyed, terrified by the thought of what he might do to her if she did not. That is why, three years before, on her twelfth birthday, (or at least twelve years from the day she had been found), when she had been told that it was time for her to begin to repay this deity for all that he had done for her, she had listened quietly and surrendered meekly to what she was certain was her solemn duty. When the first man had walked toward her in the open courtyard and tossed the silver coin at her feet, she had quietly allowed him to do what he wanted to her young body.

It was only after he was done with her that she had chanced to look up at his face. It was then that she had seen in his eyes something that had made her shudder, and she was suddenly aware that this ritual which was supposed to be a duty performed for Baal had not been just a religious experience for this man. Athalia's young heart had burned with anger.

At the time she had not been able to define what it was that had enraged her so much. She later knew that it was pure and evil lust, and it was with this revelation that her reverence for Baal had begun to dissolve into bitter hatred. Who was Baal but a convenient excuse for men to use her body as they wished?

And anyone who argued that this act was helping to convince the "great and wonderful Baal" to send suitable weather had evidently not looked outside the temple for three years. It had not rained once since she had been coerced into this detestable profession. The irony of it made her laugh out loud.

Athalia's gaze fell to her stomach, and the burning hatred in her eyes melted into pained love for the tiny child she suspected was resting there. She had considered running away from this wretched place many times in the past three years but had always resigned herself to the bitter knowledge that she had no place else to go and that she probably deserved this wretched life. Now she was becoming more and more certain there was another life to consider.

Her eyes once again flew to the representation of Baal, and then back to her stomach. Suddenly, with stubborn resolve, she knew what she must do.

∿

Hannah sat in a puddle of sunlight grinding the barley for the day's bread. Beads of sweat formed on her brow as she pressed the grinding stone roughly into the pile of grains sitting on the stone quern.

Behind her, in the corner of the courtyard, the mother ewe lay quietly in the shade that the upper floor of the house offered, her tiny offspring asleep by her side. It had been decided that the ewe and lamb would stay in the house, for now, so that the food intake of the nursing mother could be closely monitored.

"It is a miracle that she was able to conceive and give birth at all," Micah had said shaking his head, "and now she needs twice what she would normally need if this little guy is going to get enough milk to survive." Then he had assigned Nathaniel the job of collecting leaves and tender branches each day from any surviving bushes he could find to supplement the meager supply of grass available in the fields.

Hannah's hands continued to mechanically press and push the stone over the rough grains of barley smoothing them out as her mind tried desperately to push down and smooth out the turbulent future. How much longer would this drought continue? What could she do to make the few pots of barley grain last? When would they need to slaughter the few remaining sheep just to stay alive? And where was Samuel? Was he alive? Would she be his wife, or was she already a widow? And did any of it really matter if they were all going to starve soon anyway?

With a sigh, Hannah set the grinding stone down to give her aching hands and mind a moment's rest. She glanced over at the little ball of wool snuggled close to his mother. Her tight face softened slightly as she saw the tiny ears flicker; the little determined life brought a sliver of hope to her anxious heart.

A noise pulled Hannah from her thoughts, and she looked up to see someone flying towards the open door of the courtyard.

"Hannah, there you are! You are just never going to believe what has happened to me! It's just perfectly dreadful!"

Hannah smiled slightly as her rather disheveled friend bounded into the courtyard and dropped to her knees to catch her breath. The words that had come tumbling from the lips of this breathless, red-faced girl were not alarming, for Rachel had always been known for her dramatic flair and tendency to talk until she ran out of breath.

But as Hannah lifted her gaze to give her friend her full attention and patiently wait for the "perfectly dreadful" story to unfold, her smile faded and her brow wrinkled in concern, for the face of her friend registered genuine distress.

For a moment Rachel simply stared down at her hands lying in her lap. Then she raised her troubled eyes to meet those of her favorite person in the world. "Father is making me marry some rich man."

Hannah waited as Rachel took a deep, slow breath before continuing. "Oh Hannah! He's so old. I just know he is over fifty, and something about him is just so very unpleasant. I can't exactly put my finger on it but . . ." She threw her hands up in the air. "Oh, maybe it's just that I have always had silly dreams of the perfect man with such a wonderful laugh. I don't think this man ever laughs. I mean, I've only seen him a few times, but he just doesn't seem the laughing sort."

Hannah looked into the troubled eyes of her dear friend and felt truly helpless. "Have you told your father how you feel?" Of course, she had, Hannah knew, for Rachel was never known to keep even the most trivial of her thoughts and concerns unexpressed, but Hannah was at a loss for words to console her distraught friend.

"Yes, I tried to talk to him, but he just sighed and got that exasperated tone in his voice and said, 'Rachel, dear, must you dramatize everything? You act as though you were the victim in some tragic myth. With this drought I am no longer able to properly provide for you and now a man who has the means to care for you for the rest of your life has graciously offered to wed you.'"

Rachel took a breath and looked pleadingly into Hannah's eyes. "Oh Hannah, I just can't marry him. It would be positively wretched!"

Hannah laid a sympathetic hand over her friend's own wringing ones.

"It was Mara's idea, Daddy's new wife." Rachel rolled her eyes. "My mother, I suppose that makes her now, but my real mother would never have let this happen. I just know it."

Rachel sighed and ran her finger absently along the ground. "Elihu, that's the man's name, is Mara's cousin or something. He is from Shechem. She just wants to be rid of me, I know, so that she has only to deal with her own children. I mean, she treats me all right I guess, but I can tell she would rather not have me hanging around. She ran into this cousin of hers in Samaria the other day. He had some business or something to conduct there, I guess, and she set the whole thing up. It did not take her long to convince

Father that this Elihu was a perfect catch. He's apparently a rich and devout Hebrew. What else could a man want for his daughter?"

Rachel sighed and dropped her eyes to the ground. Hannah put an arm around her sad friend, as they sat in silence for a few moments.

Suddenly Rachel's eyes shot up again to meet Hannah's and her hand flew to her mouth. "Oh, what a terrible friend I am! Here I am going on and on lost in my own misery, and I completely forgot to ask you how you are doing!"

"All is well," was Hannah's quiet reply.

~

Now that the decision had been made, Athalia felt a fluttering giddiness with the excitement of escaping this place. Escaping this life. She knew it would be far from easy, but she had to get out of there one way or another. For the child.

Her heart racing, Athalia glanced around the courtyard to see if anyone was paying attention to her. Everyone was busily going about their daily duties. She clutched the wooden flute tightly to her chest. If only she could get into the inner room of the temple without anyone noticing, she was sure that she could get out while everyone was busy in the courtyard.

Taking a deep breath, Athalia gathered all her courage and stepped forward. Being careful to walk slowly and evenly across the courtyard, head down so that any observer would not read the anxious excitement and fear mingled together on her face, she headed for the inner room of the temple. She was a mere ten feet from her destination when the gentle thud of a coin at her feet jerked her out of her intense concentration.

The flute dropped out of her hand as her head flung up to see the one from whom the silver had appeared. There stood the leering face of one who filled her heart with deep disgust. Her hands rose to her stomach as though to protect the child from the hideously familiar form before them.

"May the goddess Astarte favor you, and Baal favor me."

The familiar words had never sounded so hollow. Athalia swallowed the contempt and disappointment she felt rise in her throat and forced a weak smile. The man laughed at her obvious discomfort. It was the same dry laugh he had laughed many times before in her presence. Athalia had never been able to hear it without shuddering at the tangible evil she felt which always accompanied the sound.

The fact that he was a Hebrew just sickened her further. A man, claiming to be the child of the supposed "one true God" coming to satisfy his own lustful desires in the house of a god who happened to approve, and even crave such actions did nothing but disgust Athalia.

She had seen many of these children of Israel toss a coin at a girl and had become convinced that their god about whom they made such claims must not be so great if his children would go to another god to have their desires met.

Well, this Hebrew was obviously determined to have his way with her and would quite unlikely be persuaded to come tomorrow instead, so Athalia braced herself against the inevitable and followed the despised figure. Her only consolation was that this would be the last time.

∾

"What was that all about?"

Hannah looked up to see Micah standing over her.

"With Rachel, I mean. I just saw her leave, and she looks depressed or something. I don't think I've ever seen her look so down."

Hannah sighed. "She is being forced to marry some man from Shechem."

"Oh." Micah looked down making patterns in the dust with his foot.

Hannah rose, laying down the grinding stone and sweeping the fresh flour into a clay pot. "I've got to go get Abbigail from Mama now. She needs some rest before she has to feed her again, and then I have to get this bread made." As she turned to go, she noted the concerned eyes staring down at the dust and added, "Don't worry about Rachel. She'll be all right."

Micah nodded as Hannah turned to go up the stairs. He leaned down to pick up the lamb who had come over to rub against his leg. He placed the lamb over his shoulders and called quietly to the mother sheep, "Come." The ewe, immediately recognizing the voice, came lumbering out from the shady corner of the courtyard and followed him out of the house.

With long quick strides Micah made his way out of the village to where the rest of the flock was waiting at the well.

"She'll be all right," Micah repeated quietly to the lamb whose soft head was rubbing against his cheek. His experience had given evidence to the truth of the statement. It was what intrigued Micah so much about their childhood friend. No matter what the crisis, Rachel always managed to smile her way through it. He remembered back to two years before when her mother had died. He knew it had torn her heart to watch as the one she loved grew so sick, and finally left this earth. Yet, it had been she who seemed to smile the most and offer the most comfort to others who had come to mourn with her.

And then when her father had remarried, Micah knew that life had grown harder still for Rachel. He knew that the three brothers and two sisters whom she had so quickly acquired through the marriage of the widows were anything but kind to her. Still, he had yet to hear a negative word about them come out of her mouth.

Micah realized that this new situation would be sure to add to her troubles. Now she would be forced to leave all she knew to live with a man she did not even know. He also knew that this was often the way it happened, a father arranging a marriage for his daughter based on convenience. But Rachel would be fine, as Hannah had said. She would find something to smile about yet again.

But would he? This news had severely upset his own plans for her future . . . and his.

Turning from his thoughts with a sigh Micah made his way through the small crowd that waited for the only remaining source of water near the village. The well had not yet run dry, and every villager who had any livestock left had come to water them. Nathaniel stood with his own small flock a short distance from the well.

"I didn't let any of them wander away," Nathaniel proclaimed proudly, waving the staff as Micah approached.

Micah laughed. "I knew you wouldn't!" He also knew, as he patted the small head and set the lamb down, that the well in the middle of the day was the best place to begin training the future shepherd. Wild animals were highly unlikely to be seen this close to the village, especially at this time of day, and the likelihood of thievery was equally slim with so many witnesses present.

"I was going to fill the trough, but Rachel said she would do it so I could keep an eye on them better."

Micah's smile faded as he looked quickly towards the well. There she was, pitcher balanced on her shoulder, walking towards them. She smiled as she approached. But Micah noticed the smile did not seem to reach her eyes today.

"Your little shepherd was doing a great job," she said to Micah as she lowered the pitcher and poured it into the stone trough. "Some days I wish my own father had sheep. I think it would be fun to be a shepherdess."

"Well you can help us out, can't she Micah?" Nathaniel beamed up at the pretty girl. "We have more sheep than usual since we are taking care of Samuel's until he gets back."

Rachel's smile faded and Micah glanced at her with a slight shrug.

"Why does everyone always get quiet and sad when I say anything about Samuel's sheep?" Nathaniel asked.

Micah knelt down, facing the boy. "Nathaniel, we don't know if Samuel is coming back. We don't know where he is or why he left."

"But Hannah says . . ."

"All is well," Rachel interrupted placing a protective hand on the boy's shoulder. "Hannah says all is well, and that he is coming back. And we hope so much that she is right. Right Micah?"

Micah looked up at the pretty, pleading face and then back to the small, confused one. Then he glanced over to the tiny lamb who had laid down at Nathaniel's feet. Shalom.

Micah rose with a sigh. "Right," he said patting the small head. "All is well."

2

"Surely He has borne our griefs and carried our sorrows; . . .
He was led as a lamb to the slaughter,"

ISAIAH 53:4A,7B (NKJV)

NATHANIEL SAT CROSS-LEGGED IN the otherwise empty courtyard with the newest addition to the flock lying in his lap. He laid his cheek against the soft, fluffy wool, and then raised his little head to stare sadly up at the clear blue sky.

"I really wish it would rain so that your mom and the other sheep could find grass to eat. Micah says it's a good thing you are a fat-tailed sheep. He said God made you to store up food for times like these, just like a camel! But you don't have a hump. You store your food in your rump! Isn't that crazy how God made you that way?"

He rubbed the fuzzy head and frowned. "But you still need some food to store up, and it has been so long since it has rained.

"Hannah says things were different before it stopped raining. I don't remember it, but she says we used to have servants to help Daddy in the fields. There were servants to cook and clean too. But not anymore. Daddy doesn't say much about it, but I see him looking up at the sky a lot and then shaking his head."

The boy shook his head slowly to illustrate his point. "I don't think he wants to worry Mama. She's sick, you know. She got sick when she had baby Abbigail, and she never got better. Mama mostly stays in bed now. She likes it when I go up and sit on her mat and tell her stories though. She laughs then. I like it when she laughs. It almost seems like she is not sick then."

Nathaniel stopped, turning his head to look up the stone staircase where he knew his mother was lying on her mat in the common sleeping area. A glistening tear rolled down his cheek. "If only baby Abbigail hadn't been born . . ."

Shalom pushed his velvety nose into the boy's chest, as though urging him on.

"It's just not fair, you know," said Nathaniel looking down at the lamb. "We were all doing fine. Mama, Daddy, Micah, Hannah, and me. Then she had to come, and now Mama doesn't even get out of bed!" Nathaniel fiercely brushed away a tear. "Why did we need her? It's not like she does anything anyway. She just lies there and sleeps a lot."

For a moment, Nathaniel was still and silent.

Just as the lamb decided to take advantage of the stillness and had wriggled himself into a comfortable position, Nathaniel slammed his fists down onto the hard dirt floor, and the lamb jumped.

"I just wish she had never been born," Nathaniel whispered.

The sun was shining brightly as Hannah entered the city this late morning to sell her tapestries. The trip to Samaria was too long to make very often, but too profitable to neglect altogether. There were smaller marketplaces nearer to her own village, but the traffic in and out of them did not compare to that of the capital city. Before the drought, servants would make the journey, taking with them Hannah's woven tapestries, barley from her father's fields, and sometimes sheep tails which were a coveted fat to use in cooking. When the drought had taken its toll on the barley and sheep, and it had become too much of a financial burden to keep the servants, her father had made the trips, but they were far fewer. It had been months since the journey had been made.

Hannah smiled at the memory of her father's nervous suggestion the evening before.

"A few families from the village are going into Samaria to-morrow morning, and I was thinking maybe you could go with them and sell the tapestries you have finished."

Hannah had looked up at him in surprise at the suggestion, knowing how much he hated the idea of his daughter going into the city, but then she had noticed the deep concern in the eyes that had met hers. She had realized then that he thought the trip would be a good distraction. Ever since that horrible night, Hannah had found herself often met by quiet, troubled looks and weak smiles. No one was quite certain what to say or do to lessen the grief and worry they knew she was feeling.

So, Hannah had risen before the sun and joined the villagers' small caravan of traders, livestock, and carts filled with wares, and headed to the big city to set up a booth in the marketplace. Located directly inside the gates, the marketplace was filled daily with these booths set up by people from all over Israel attempting to earn their living, though the drought had severely dwindled the number of both buyers and sellers.

But as Hannah entered the city this morning, she realized that her father had been right. It was a good distraction. She enjoyed the exercise, and today she was particularly enjoying the feel of the sunshine on her face. Hannah was aware that the sun's rays were not a source of enjoyment to most of the adult population this morning, and even many of the small children of the land had begun to realize the dreadful significance of each day free of rain clouds. She knew that the dirt on which she trod desperately needed a good soaking, but still she could not find it in herself to dislike the bright light of the sun, unhampered by clouds. She had always loved sunny days. It was hard to feel truly depressed while observing God's creation by the revitalizing light of that huge flame in the sky. Hannah smiled to herself, remembering the words of her little brother: "Hannah, isn't it nice of God to get up so early every morning and push up the sun? I wonder, do you think it is very heavy for him?"

Well, it was nice of God, and Hannah was quite thankful this morning for that intensely bright light which helped, somehow, to ease the gnawing pain and worry that crept up from her stomach no matter how determined she was to keep it pushed down. She was almost inside the city gates when the thankfulness in her heart pushed its way up to her mouth and burst out into a short laugh as her hands lifted to the sky. "Thank you, God, for getting up this morning to lift the sun into its place!"

In the next moment a sudden movement caught Hannah's attention and she dropped her hands. It was there in the shadow of a small enclave in the wall right next to the gate. Hannah raised a hand to shade her eyes as a small figure came into focus, crouched low, as if hiding. Stepping towards the wall, Hannah noticed the figure was that of a girl close to her own age. Her body was shaking slightly, and her eyes were full of fear. Hannah smiled at her, and for just a moment, their eyes locked. Then, just as suddenly, the girl turned her head, and scrambled out of the shadow into the mass of people inside the gate. The tinkling sound that accompanied the flight brought Hannah's attention to a flash of silver near the girl's bare foot which extended out from under the tunic as she ran.

Hurrying forward, Hannah pushed through the crowd, trying to keep sight of the girl, but soon lost her in the chaos.

"What kind of trouble is that poor girl in to be hiding in the shadows like a frightened animal?" whispered Hannah to herself looking intently into the crowd ahead of her. Realizing that the girl had disappeared with no desire to be found, Hannah breathed a prayer for the distraught stranger and gave up her search. But the gentle tinkling of the ankle bracelet remained in her ears the rest of the day.

∽

Athalia sat down in a vacant alley to catch her breath. She put her hands over her eyes and shook her head. "Why am I running like a frightened child?" she wondered to herself with disgust.

She leaned over to detach the slender silver chains around her ankles. Athalia had grabbed a tunic on her way out of the temple to cover her own scant apparel, but in her haste to leave, she had forgotten about the anklets. As she looked down at the chains, she paused, recalling how temple life in her younger days had intrigued her. The constant activity and what seemed to her like endless parties were a source of great excitement for the young girl. As a child, she had watched the older girls, a bit envious of their exotic apparel and tinkling ankle bracelets as they danced for the many men who came to watch them. But now, as she stared down at the chains, they seemed no less oppressive than those that would bind a prisoner.

Throwing them from her, she sighed in exasperation and drew her thoughts back to the present. And to the strange girl who had so thoroughly unnerved her.

"What was she doing anyway," she muttered, "throwing her hands up in the air like that?"

There Athalia stopped. She shook her head. It was not the hands thrown into the air that had troubled her. It was the eyes. The eyes that had met hers for just an instant had seemed both genuinely joyful and sincerely concerned about Athalia, a total stranger. They were smiling eyes.

Athalia shivered in spite of the heat. She drew her knees to her chest and sat, staring, unseeing, at the mud brick wall across from her, unaware of the hot tears that were falling onto the wooden flute in her lap.

~

Nathaniel leaned back from a pile of rocks he had just cleared from the dry hillside. He pushed back his hair, damp from sweat, to watch as the sickle in his father's hand swished back and forth, cutting away long sections of vine.

"Are there going to be enough vines left for any grapes to grow on?" he asked as the pile of vines at his father's feet grew bigger and bigger.

Joseph laughed and paused long enough to take a drink from the skin bag around his waist. "Yes, Nathaniel. There will be vines for the grapes to grow on, but they will be strong new vines." He paused and looked up. "That is, if it ever rains again."

"Daddy, do you think God doesn't like us anymore? Do think that is why he isn't giving us rain?"

Joseph set the sickle on the ground and sat down beside the boy. "Nathaniel, do you remember me telling you about my grandfather, and how he would always tell me stories about what God did for the Israelites after he rescued them from Egypt?"

"Yes, Daddy. I know all the stories."

"Well, I remember him telling me once that one of the things God told Moses to tell the Israelites was that they needed to listen carefully and follow all of his instructions. He said that if they served God and followed his instructions, he would give them rain, both the early rain that comes before planting, and the latter rain that comes in the spring before harvest. But he told them to be careful, because if they decided to stop serving him, and start serving other gods, he would shut up the heavens and there would be no more rain." [1]

"But we serve him, Daddy," Nathaniel said cocking his head quizzically.

"I know, son, but there aren't many Israelites who do any more. Most people have forgotten the stories of what God did for us, and they don't care anymore. Even my own father didn't serve God. He had us go to the temple in Samaria when I was little to offer sacrifices to Baal. All of the stories I tell you are the ones I remember my grandfather telling me."

Nathaniel considered that for a moment. "Why don't you serve Baal like your dad?"

"I loved my father, very much, but he never seemed happy to me. He didn't smile much, and he always seemed worried or troubled about something. And when we went to the temple in Samaria, I always felt that same way; like something wasn't right. My grandfather gave me the opposite feeling. He was always smiling and laughing. He always answered my questions and had a sort of peace around him. When I asked him about it, he said it was because he trusted that God would always take care of him, so he didn't have anything to worry about. He said that all the stories, the

1. See Deuteronomy 11:13–17

same ones I have told you, gave him evidence of a great God who cared about his people. After he died, I remember thinking that I wanted to be like my grandfather. I wanted that same peace he had. So, I repeated all of the stories he told me to myself and anyone else who would listen, and I discovered that the more I repeated the stories, the more I believed that my grandfather was right. If God would take care of his people like that, I can trust him to take care of me."

"Did your dad get mad?"

"No, he didn't care if I wanted to serve God. He still made the trip to Jerusalem every so often to do what he thought it was his duty to do as an Israelite. You could say he served both Baal and God. But neither very strongly."

Nathaniel looked up at the cloudless sky. "So . . . God is mad at Israel, and we don't get any rain because of it."

"He is certainly not happy with the way things are going in Israel," Joseph said following his son's gaze heavenward, "but I'm not sure it is accurate to say he is not sending rain because he is mad. When I discipline you, it is not because I am mad, but because I want to keep you well and safe."

"Like when I got a whipping last week for going to look for Micah without telling you where I was going?"

Joseph smiled. "Exactly like that. You know I tell you to stay near the house unless someone knows where you are going. That is my rule. I don't make rules because I like to make a list of things to control you. I want you to be safe, and if I don't know where you are, I can't keep you safe. Anything could have happened to you, and no one would have even known where to look to find you. It hurts to get a whipping, but my hope is that, because you remember the pain of the rod, you will not disobey and end up getting hurt far worse."

Nathaniel raised his eyes. "But if God doesn't give us rain, we will starve. How could we get hurt worse than that?"

"There are things worse than death here on earth, Nathaniel," Joseph said quietly, placing a hand on the boy's shoulder. "God is more concerned with the condition of our hearts than the condition of our bodies. The condition of our heart affects not only us, but all the people who will be born after we die. And I suspect there is something eternal about our hearts. I suspect that the condition of our heart affects our eternity."

"Eternity. That means forever, right?"

Joseph nodded, "Yes, and I think that the drought might make people think about what God said and start taking a look at their own hearts."

"You shall love the LORD your God with all your heart, with all your soul, and with all your strength,"[2] Nathaniel whispered, quoting the words of Moses.

"Good memory, Son," Joseph said with a smile. "Yes, that is one of the things God told Moses. It is the most important thing, I suspect."

"Well, at least one thing good comes of it not raining," Nathaniel said standing up and wiping the dust off his tunic.

"What is that, Son?"

"There aren't many weeds to pull around these grape vines this year!"

Joseph laughed and gave the boy's head a rub. "But there is still plenty to do! There are still rocks to clear away, and we have to get this terrace wall repaired just in case God decides to send rain before the grape harvest."

Nathaniel looked up to the sky again and sighed. "I sure hope he does."

Joseph stood up and studied his son's face, so serious and thoughtful as he gazed up into the heavens. Then he said, "You know, Son, there is someone I want you to see tomorrow."

～

The flute dropped from her mouth. Not even the sweet sound of the tiny instrument could calm Athalia's troubled heart this evening.

"What have I done?" She looked down at her swelling belly and laid her hand on it. "I am so very sorry little one. I just could

2. Deuteronomy 6:5 (NKJV)

not bear the thought of you growing up in the service of that horrible thing they call a god. But now look. Here we are, half a day's journey from the city gates, all alone with nothing, no food, or even a blanket to keep us warm. What was I thinking?"

Athalia drew her knees up to her chin. Silently the tears began to drop from the wide eyes. "Maybe we should return . . ."

A shudder ran through her as she spoke the words. What would that mean? For her? For the baby?

Asdrubal had warned her about getting pregnant. "Don't forget to drink the tea!" she would admonish often. Asdrubal had become pregnant once and had been forced to take certain herbs to abort the baby early on. Athalia remembered that day well. It was the only day she had ever seen Asdrubal without a smile.

Athalia was not yet twelve when she had found Asdrubal outside the court, curled up in fetal position and rocking back and forth. "What happened?" the young Athalia had asked innocently. The eyes staring back at her did not seem to see her at all. "It was so tiny and helpless . . ." were the whispered words of response.

No. She could not return to the temple.

Athalia looked around at the dry, cracked earth surrounding her. The few juniper trees that had managed to draw what little water the earth had held for the past few years were all the landscape that surrounded her for miles it seemed.

She needed water for herself and the child, but it had not rained for three years and was unlikely to do so now just for her. A tear ran down her cheek as she realized that death would likely be the outcome. She did not much care about herself, but this child had come to mean everything to her, and it grieved her to think about its death.

"I am sorry my dear child. All I wanted was to protect you from that . . . that evil. But through no fault of your own, you were conceived out of evil. It is my fault. I am so sorry. I wish I could undo it all. I knew even three years ago there was something not right about it, yet at the time it all seemed so exciting. The music, the dancing . . . But then after that first man had . . ." She shuddered at the memory.

"Then, after I realized how detestable the whole thing was, I was ashamed. Ashamed and afraid. There was no going back. I couldn't undo anything. I would never be pure again. And now you, dear child, will suffer and there is nothing I can do to undo that either. If only there was some magic to undo all the wrongs . . ."

Athalia closed her eyes and leaned her head back against the struggling juniper tree which had been a slight refuge for herself and her unborn child from the burning rays of the sun during the day.

"There is nothing I can do to undo it all . . ." As the words left her dry lips, Athalia felt herself surrendering to whatever fate awaited them.

As she pondered this, she became suddenly aware of the irony of her situation; as she sat there facing likely death, she felt more peace than she had ever felt before. For the first evening that she could remember, she did not feel the oppressive evil of that place that had been her home for so long. She felt only sorrow for the child.

But then her mind wandered to her own participation in the evil, and shame washed over her, taking with it a bit of the peace that had seemed to be telling her all would be well.

Athalia laid down on her side, one hand on her belly and the other behind her head hoping to sleep in order to escape the shame and sorrow that had once more settled down upon her. As she lay there gazing toward the horizon, she could see the sun slowly descending to its own place of rest. It was leaving behind layers of soft color which blended into the approaching night.

Such beauty amidst so much evil. Or was it the other way around?

The friendly lights of the stars began to appear, as the deep blue of the night pushed the sun still further over the horizon. The stars seemed to dance and laugh, inviting Athalia to take part in the joy of nightfall, and Athalia began to feel a bit of the peace return. Her eyelids slowly fell, and she entered a deep sleep where she was met with joyful dreams of riding shooting stars and dancing on the moon with her child in her arms.

∽

Rachel sat silently beside her friend, infuriated by the two girls who had shrugged and walked away from them. She saw them whispering to each other and glancing back at them as they balanced the jugs of water on their heads.

"Just concerned," they had said. But Rachel knew differently. They had wanted a bit of gossip. An "update" on the situation which had been the talk of the village ever since that dreadful night.

But in her fury, Rachel could find no suitable words for either the snooping girls or her beautifully composed friend sitting quietly beside her on the edge of the well.

"He will come," had been the quiet words that Hannah had replied to the girls' inquiries. Rachel wanted so badly to believe that for her friend.

She looked down at the well on which they sat. "Have you ever thought about how Rebeccah felt all those years ago?"

Hannah looked up with a quizzical smile, waiting for her friend to explain the seemingly random question. "Rebeccah?"

"Yeah, Jacob and Esau's mother. You know, Isaac's wife."

Hannah laughed. "Go on."

"Well, here we are, sitting on a well, wondering and worrying about our future husbands, and I was thinking about how Rebeccah must have felt to be going to the well one day, just like she always did, and then some strange man with lots of camels comes by and tells her that she has been chosen by God to be the wife of some man she has never met."

"It was probably at least a little frightening I suppose," Hannah offered.

"Yeah! A little!" Rachel laughed. "But chosen by God. That has to be something, to be told that God picked you to be the specific wife for a specific man . . . who turned out to be the father of a whole nation!"

Hannah smiled. She was used to her friend's endless streams of thought and knew there would somehow be a point eventually.

"I just wish," she said quietly, "I just wish I could know I was chosen by God to be somebody's wife. If I knew God chose me to be Elihu's wife, then I could bear it better, even if it was scary and hard."

~

Hannah hopped down off the well as she watched Rachel walk away with a pot of water balanced on her shoulder. Slowly she picked up her own pot as her friend's words echoed through her mind: "I just wish I could know I was chosen by God to be somebody's wife."

Hannah glanced up towards the sky, and then quickly and deliberately turned her body towards the house and her mind to the evening meal she would need to prepare.

But she was not quick enough.

Thoughts of her betrothed slipped in through the cracks of the fortress Hannah had begun to build that horrible night.

He had promised he would come for her that day, but there was no promise of exactly when. "Surely he has just been detained by some last-minute business," she had assured her mother whose wrinkled brow had attested to worry as the night grew longer and longer. And so, they had waited. All night they had waited, dressed and ready.

But he had not come.

Her friends had all waited with her at first, but throughout the night the number of friends had decreased, so that by dawn, only Rachel had remained with her. She had remained until late morning when Micah had come with the news that Samuel had disappeared.

People whispered that maybe he had become frightened at the thought of marriage. Maybe he had found another. But Hannah knew that neither could be true. She knew her Samuel. They had grown up together, the closest of friends, and the time they had spent together had built a trust that would not easily be broken. She had given her heart to this man, and she trusted him with it completely, even now. He would be back for her if it were at all possible. But was it possible?

She began to walk faster, willing the worry away, but it would not be dismissed. She told herself she would not deal with this now. There was too much to do. She was the stable one. She had to keep things going while her mother could not. She could not break . . .

She was running now as quickly as she could manage with a pot of water on her shoulder. No! Not tears! She brushed at the stream of dampness that was blurring her vision. She would not allow this to overwhelm her . . .

But it was too late.

Hannah sank down onto her knees and dropped the pot, hands cupped over her bowed face catching the tears which were now steadily dropping from her lashes as she gave in to the grief and despair which enclosed and threatened to smother her. Dropping her fists to beat them on the hard, dry ground, and throwing back her head, she shouted, "Why? Why, God? What have you done with my Samuel? It's not fair! I should be his wife right now, and I don't even know if he is alive! God? What are you doing?"

She was hitting the ground with a fierceness that was bruising her knuckles, and her sobs shook every inch of her slender form. After some time, exhaustion took over, and Hannah fell limply to the ground, face down, completely spent.

Lying there, still shaking from the intensity of the sobs, her thoughts, jumbled from the weight of the emotion, began to settle themselves.

She looked up at the sky. The sun was setting and shades of red and purple stretched across the horizon in perfect harmony. The beauty and peacefulness of it seemed to mock her hurting heart, intensifying, for a moment, the frustration with the creator who made it so.

"It just isn't fair," she whispered.

In the silence of the evening, she could hear Nathaniel laughing in the distance. He was still playing with that sweet little lamb.

Hannah had begun to suspect that that same sweet little lamb would be the one offered as a sacrifice in a few weeks when they traveled to Jerusalem: perfect, without blemish.

What was fair about that?

Slowly, as she lay there, the illusion of a mocking God faded into all she knew of the maker of the universe. This God, the one who had created the color that splashed so gloriously across the evening sky, the one who had created an entire universe and she within it, this God was a holy God: perfect, without blemish. He deserved from his creation absolute honor and devotion and received far less, yet still he chose to graciously bend to lead and protect the very ones who continually offended him. This was a God with power greater than can be imagined and with every right to destroy those who snubbed him time and time again, and yet, mercifully, he did not, asking only that a lamb without spot be offered to him as a reminder that something had to be punished for the offenses of the offenders.

Hannah lifted herself onto her elbow and shaded her eyes with her hand to look out across the field. She could barely make out the running form of the boy and the lamb who chased after him. That innocent lamb would die instead of her, and yet here she lay telling God what was and was not fair. The irony of it almost made her smile. Almost.

"Thank God life is not fair," Hannah whispered softly.

Micah held his staff over the entrance of the sheepfold, counting as he ran the staff over the course wool of each sheep to check for bugs and sores as they entered, one by one.

Twelve lean sheep.

Micah shook his head slowly as he sat down at the entrance and prepared to settle in for the night. The drought had simultaneously decreased the number of sheep and raised the number of hungry men willing to resort to thievery to fill their grumbling bellies. It was more important than ever to guard the small flock through the night, and long gone were the days of being able to afford to hire someone to do it for him. About a year into the drought, Micah and Samuel had decided to combine their dwindling flocks and share the duties. But there was no sharing now.

The evening was chilly, and Micah wrapped himself tightly in the wool mantle as he looked intently far out past the village. "What happened to you, my friend?" he whispered into the stillness.

His mind wandered back to that morning last week. He had been gathering the sheep to take them to the fields when his dearest friend had come running across the fields towards him.

"I need you to gather everyone and be ready tonight."

Micah smiled as he recalled the sheepish grin that had accompanied the words.

"I have something I need to do today, but I will be back by sunset. Be ready. And let Hannah know."

Micah's smile faded at the memory. "If only I had asked him what he was doing, where he was going. Then maybe there would be some clue . . ."

Over and over Micah recalled the details of that evening and the following day. The companions of the groom had been collected and were waiting at Samuel's house all night. When he had not returned by dawn, the companions had gone home leaving Micah, the chosen friend of the bridegroom, to deliver the news to Hannah.

Micah had spent that entire day asking around in the village and searching the surrounding area on foot. It was not until late that night that he had returned alone, discouraged, and tired. The bridegroom was missing. Gone. Vanished. And now Micah alone was responsible for the twelve hungry sheep.

∽

The little lamb ran towards the door when he saw the boy enter the courtyard.

"Shalom!" Nathaniel cried as he knelt to embrace the lamb. "Guess what! Tomorrow Daddy is taking me to see Elijah! You know, the great man of God? King Ahab and his mean wife Jezebel hate him. Daddy says it's because they can't get him no matter how hard they try. Jezebel already had all the prophets of the true God killed . . . or the ones she could find anyway. She only wants her evil prophets around who tell her stuff she wants to hear. But she could not get Elijah!"

Nathaniel drew his shoulders back, straight and serious, proud of the man he had heard so much about.

"Jezebel worships Baal, you know," Nathaniel solemnly informed the wriggling lamb in his arms. "He's not the one true God, you know. Our God is the true God. He made everything there is! Even you, Shalom!"

Nathaniel lifted the lamb up to his face and nuzzled the soft nose and then sat him back down on his lap. "I guess King Ahab and Queen Jezebel don't know about the true God, 'cause they built a bunch of stuff to worship Baal. They even built a whole temple for him in Samaria where they live! Daddy says Israel used to be a nation that served the real God. But there have been a lot of kings lately that don't pay much attention to what the real God says. Daddy says that they had better be scared, because God won't put up with it much longer, he thinks. He thinks that's why there hasn't been rain for so long.

"Anyway, Elijah still loves God, and now he told everyone in Israel to go up some mountain tomorrow for something. No one is sure what. But Daddy said I could go with him! I get to see Elijah! I think he is probably the most famous man in Israel, except maybe for King Ahab himself, and no one has seen him for a really long time. Daddy says he heard that Elijah even made somebody who was dead come back to life! Wow! I wonder what he is going to do tomorrow!"

3

"These will make war with the Lamb, and the Lamb will overcome
them, for He is Lord of lords and King of kings; and those who are
with Him are called, chosen, and faithful."

REVELATION 17:14 (NKJV)

A GREAT COMMOTION WOKE Athalia from her deep sleep.
Unconsciously, she threw a protective hand over her belly. She
propped herself up on her elbow, shading her eyes from the blind-
ing light of the morning sun which reflected off the dry earth and
wondered at the sight that greeted her. There, coming toward her
from the direction of the city, were more people than she could
count, all in an obvious hurry to be somewhere. But where? She
had not the slightest notion how far she had traveled the day before, and had, therefore, no idea where she was.

"Why would so many people be headed away from the city so
early in the day?" she wondered aloud groggily.

Glancing around, she saw that there were already a great
many people behind her. "I must have been really exhausted to
have slept through the first part of such a migration," she muttered
to herself.

Athalia started to rise, but a wave of dizziness pushed her back
against the tree by which she had slept. She sank to the ground,
dropped her pulsating head into her hands, and fought desperately

the whirlpool of her mind that seemed to pull her spinning downward into the black unconsciousness below.

After a moment or two of gripping pain, the spinning began to slow, and Athalia's vision began to clear. She had not had food or water for a day and a half now. Slowly, Athalia dropped her hands and lifted her still swimming head to the crowds which were quickly approaching. What was going on? It must be something of significance in order to draw what looked like all of Israel from daily business. But what could it possibly be?

As the crowds drew nearer, Athalia sat up to listen, hoping to catch snatches of conversation which might give some idea as to their destination. This was not a difficult task, for all were so deeply intent on whatever it was that was driving them away from their daily routine that it was upon this that all conversation revolved, and no one seemed to notice the girl sitting under the tree.

"That's what I was told. It must be something big for King Ahab himself to go along with it. You know how he hates Elijah."

". . . and I heard that the prophets of Baal will all be there too! How odd . . ."

". . . but why Mount Carmel?"

"Mount Carmel," whispered Athalia to herself. "But that's got to be at least thirty miles from the city gates! How far did I get yesterday?"

By this time there were so many people hurrying past that it was getting difficult to decipher complete ideas from any one conversation, and Athalia's head began to spin once more with the effort of concentration. She closed her eyes as, once again, the nauseous dizziness pressed upon her. She was just about to give in to the whirlpool which was pulling her from consciousness when she felt a gentle pressure on her shoulder.

"Are you all right?" The voice was soft and filled with concern, and somehow familiar.

Athalia struggled to pull herself from the whirlpool, and with great effort opened her eyes. Slowly, the kneeling form in front of her came into focus: the long silky black hair pulled back into one long braid, the delicate features, the concerned eyes . . .

Suddenly Athalia gasped as recognition struck like lightning. "You're the girl who was laughing into the sky," she whispered with great effort.

Hannah smiled, her suspicion that this was the frightened girl she had seen at the city gate having just been confirmed. "Are you feeling all right? You look rather ill."

Trying desperately to push away the fuzz from her confused mind, Athalia could only shake her head.

"Here. Have some water." Hannah opened the jug she had been carrying and tipped it to the lips of the thirsty girl.

Athalia sipped it gratefully and then leaned her head back closing her eyes once again. Maybe this was all a dream . . . this girl with the smiling eyes . . . giving her water . . . she had heard of strange visions seen by those who were dying of thirst . . .

But things seemed to be clearing now rather than fading. She opened her eyes. The girl was still there. It was no illusion. There were those eyes, still watching intently. Suddenly Athalia remembered the crowds passing by.

"Where is everyone going?" she asked weakly.

"To Mount Carmel," replied Hannah, placing her hand on the forehead of the girl to check for fever. "King Ahab sent a strange message throughout Israel for everyone to go to Mount Carmel. No one quite understands what it is about, except that it was apparently at the request of Elijah, the prophet of the one true God."

"The one true God?" Athalia tilted her head. "You mean the one you were thanking the other day?"

Hannah smiled and nodded her head.

Athalia thought about all the men claiming to be servants of the one true God who had thrown a coin her way over the years. None of them had eyes like this girl.

"The prophets of Baal are supposed to be there too," Hannah continued.

The sudden stiffening at the mention of Baal did not go unnoticed by Hannah. She changed the subject. "Where do you live?"

The silent stare which greeted the question made Hannah quite unsure that this subject was much safer.

Hannah turned her attention to the bag she was carrying. "I'm sorry. That is none of my business. Here. Have some more water and a bit of bread. I baked it fresh this morning."

The two sat in silence for a few minutes as Athalia sipped and nibbled gratefully.

After a while, Hannah rose to her feet. "Do you feel well enough to make the trip to Mount Carmel to see what the fuss is about? It's only another three or four miles from here. I would love the company and I just do not feel at all good about leaving you here alone feeling as you do. My father and brothers went on ahead. I told them I would meet them, if I can find them in the crowd that is, but I really do not want to leave you here alone. Will you come?"

Athalia was not sure how to respond. She looked up into the friendly eyes and knew the offer was made in complete sincerity. Yet why would this strange girl take such an interest in an obvious fugitive?

"Well, whatever the motive," she thought to herself, "there is really nothing to lose in the venture." So, Athalia took the outstretched hand, and she too rose, but a bit more slowly, not wanting to face the dizziness again.

~

The crowd that had gathered atop Mount Carmel was growing restless. The people had formed a circle around a large altar already prepared with wood, and what seemed to be the remains of a smaller altar. The prophets of Baal stood murmuring together near the large altar where two oxen were tied.

Athalia stood with Hannah near the front of the crowd. She smiled slightly as Hannah reached over to grab her hand, sensing that this girl with the smiling eyes had made it her mission today to make everything all right. Athalia did not mind. It felt kind of nice to have someone care, even if it was a total stranger.

They had not been able to find Hannah's father and brothers in the crowd, but this did not bother Athalia either, for she did not relish the idea of meeting any men any time soon.

Athalia stood on her toes to see over the heads in front of her. She desperately wanted to catch a glimpse of whatever was about to happen.

Then she saw him. He was a rather odd-looking man, very hairy, with a leather belt around his waist. Not the sort you would expect to see in any high position, and yet when he came into the center of the circle, a hush fell across the crowd as all waited in anxious anticipation for whatever was to follow.

Elijah. It was the name she had heard often mentioned in the temple with haughty contempt, and now here he stood with the attention of all of Israel. Then he spoke:

"How long will you falter between two opinions?"[1] His voice was filled with grief and frustration. "If the LORD is God, follow Him; But if Baal, follow him."[2]

Athalia glanced around to see the reaction of the people around her. She recognized a few of the men as those who had come into the temple to use her services, and she knew exactly what Elijah was talking about. Many Hebrew men had come to lay with prostitutes of Baal, but none of them with whom she had come into contact had ever been willing to give up calling themselves children of the God of Israel. She noticed that some of these men had their heads bowed a bit, as if shamed by these words of Elijah, while some just stared back in contempt, but not one answered a word.

"What can they say?" Athalia laughed to herself. "He is right, whether or not they like it."

Elijah was speaking again: "I alone am left a prophet of the LORD; but Baal's prophets are four hundred and fifty men. Therefore let them give us two bulls; and let them choose one bull for themselves, cut it in pieces, and lay it on the wood, but put no fire under it; and I will prepare the other bull, and lay it on the wood, but put no fire under it. Then you call on the name of your gods,

---

1. 1 Kings 10:21a (NKJV)
2. 1 Kings 18:21b (NKJV)

and I will call on the name of the LORD; and the God who answers by fire, He is God."[3]

This seemed like a reasonable idea to Athalia, although she highly doubted whether either god would answer. The murmur of the crowd told her that others also found it acceptable. She looked up to gauge Hannah's response. Hannah's gaze was fixed on the prophet. Athalia smiled at the spark of joyous anticipation she found in those eyes which had alarmed and fascinated her so. What was it about this girl that she should laugh into the sun and pick up stray girls by the side of the road? She could not begin to guess, but whatever it was, Athalia was sure it could be found in those eyes if one was to search them deeply enough.

She looked back to Elijah who had turned to the prophets of Baal to begin the preparation of the sacrifice. She watched as the ox was slaughtered and cut into pieces. It was an all too familiar sight, having observed the procedures in the temple almost daily since her childhood, and the gore of it had long ago ceased to affect her. Today, however, as though the child inside her was fighting the gruesome image, she could feel that old, queasy feeling seeping into her stomach, and she had to turn away for fear she would be ill. She felt Hannah's hand on her shoulder and looked up to see the now familiar concern reflected in her eyes.

"I'll be fine," Athalia whispered. "My stomach has just been a bit restless recently."

"Just let me know if you want to leave," Hannah whispered back.

Athalia nodded. She knew with certainty, however, that this would not happen, for whatever was to happen to her, she needed to see what would come of this test Elijah had proposed. Her life had taught her to look quite cynically upon the higher powers that were supposed to control events, and this test would surely prove to justify her skepticism. Yet, somehow, she found that something deep inside of her wanted desperately for it to not turn out as she expected.

---

3. 1 Kings 18:22b–24a (NKJV)

Rachel stood beside her father, fascinated by the events un-
folding before her eyes. The prophets of Baal had long since lain
the pieces of the ox upon the altar and had been calling to Baal
for the fire to consume the sacrifice for hours now. Their solemn
cries had turned into fervent pleadings and wails after the first half
hour, and now they were leaping and bounding around the altar,
attempting to capture the attention of the god. It was a rather amusing sight to Rachel, and she wrapped her head covering across her
face to hide the smile.

Rachel glanced across the crowd to where the man stood to
whom she was to be wed. His face, usually twisted into a sorry
attempt at a smile, had remained expressionless throughout the
events of the morning. It was certainly not a face she wished to see
first thing every morning, and she winced at the thought. It was
not so much an unpleasant looking face as a vacant one, lined a bit
and framed with a gray beard that betrayed his years. His eyes were
the most disappointing feature for Rachel. They held not a spark
of humor or joy. For that matter, they seemed to hold nothing, or
maybe, Rachel decided cocking her head a bit, it was not what was
absent from them, but what was hidden behind them that bothered her so very much.

Rachel sighed and dropped her gaze quickly, not wanting to
be caught staring. The thought of spending every night of her life
lying beside this joyless man sent her stomach whirling in nauseous patterns.

She quickly returned her attention to the wailing prophets,
still leaping frantically about the altar. She had been studying their
faces, faces which had remained so intent in the wails and cries,
mouths either opened wide emitting a piercing wail or pressed
closed in a moan, brows drawn together until they almost met over
the nose, and the eyes so joyless, so . . .

Rachel gasped and threw her hand over her mouth as the
horror of it struck her. Elihu's eyes! They held the very same look!
Suddenly a picture of Elihu leaping and flailing ridiculously with

the four-hundred or so prophets flashed across her mind, and she felt her lips stretch involuntarily into a wide grin. She fought back the laughter which she could feel bubbling up into her throat, and Rachel was grateful for the humorous image which had, for the moment, successfully pushed all unpleasant thoughts from her mind.

"Rachel, have you seen Hannah?" The voice jerked her from her thoughts, and she jumped.

"Oh, Micah. I didn't realize you were here. No, I have not seen your sister. Didn't she come with you?"

"Yes . . . I mean no . . . I mean we lost her on the way here." The abruptness with which the words were spoken caught Rachel off guard. Micah had been one of her dearest friends for as long as she could remember. When her own mother had died, she had spent most of her time at Hannah's house and had grown to think of herself as part of the family. But lately Micah had been acting strangely toward her.

"You lost her?"

The dark, handsome, face, pinched in concern was avoiding her eyes. "We were all walking together, the servants, Father, Nathaniel, Hannah, and myself, and suddenly Hannah said something about seeing some girl she thought she knew. She said she would meet us here, and then she just took off. I turned around to see where she was going, but there were so many people I just lost her in the crowd."

Rachel smiled sadly at the loving concern for his sister in the downcast eyes. Why could not Elihu have those kinds of eyes? "Oh, you know Hannah. She will be fine. In fact, she is usually the one making it fine for everyone else!"

∾

"Are you sure you don't want to leave?" Hannah asked, bending to give the girl some water.

Athalia shook her head in answer. It was almost noon now, and she had long since sat down to view the events from a less dizzying position. Her head was aching beyond anything she had ever imagined, but she was not going to miss this. Besides, where was she going to go? She looked back up at her new friend. Could she call her that? Friend? They had finally exchanged names, so did that make them friends now?

Yes. Athalia knew she could call her friend. But now she dreaded the questions that would inevitably come. What could she tell her? That she was a runaway temple prostitute with child? She shook her head again knowing that she could not. Despairing at the thought, she directed her attention once more to the events at hand.

The prophets of Baal were still dancing around the altar as they had all morning, and Elijah, by this time, had begun to mock them. "Cry aloud, for he is a god; either he is meditating, or he is busy, or he is on a journey, or perhaps he is sleeping and must be awakened."[4]

Athalia shook her head at the sight of the hundreds of prophets yelling louder in response to Elijah's taunts. She had often heard those very excused from the temple priests as to why Baal was seeming to ignore them. They sounded so ridiculous to the observer watching the futile flailing of the men, but the devoted prophets thought them to be completely plausible explanations for the inattentions of their, very likely, busy god. After all, he had a whole universe to run.

A loud gasp beside her pulled Athalia from her thoughts. She looked down to see her new friend had fallen to her knees beside her, eyes wide in horror, her hand covering her mouth. "They . . . they are slashing themselves! Blood . . . everywhere . . ." The distraught eyes clasped shut to escape the image.

Athalia glanced up to see what had so horrified her friend and smiled grimly. Yes, it was true. Athalia had seen it all too many times before. When yelling and dancing failed to bring forth a divine answer (as was most often the case) the worshippers of Baal would often resort to self-inflicted wounds to bring about sympathy from the god. There they were, still yelling, but now in pain as they pulled out their lancets and knives, slashing their own bodies until blood was gushing out. It was a scene too familiar to produce much of a response in Athalia, but she remembered the shock of the first time she had witnessed such self-mutilation, and

---

4. 1 Kings 18:27b (NKJV)

she gazed sympathetically back at Hannah. Slowly, carefully, she placed a comforting hand on the back of the bent form beside her whose head was down, still refusing to look upon the sight. Athalia smiled. Now who was comforting whom?

$\sim$

Rachel absently nibbled on a piece of bread left over from lunch, staring down the hill in the direction of the city. She could just barely make out the lines of Samaria's wall in the distance. Nearer, she spotted the tiny dots that made up their own village. She covered her mouth to stifle a yawn. It had been a long trip to the mount, but most of the village had decided to make it in one day, so it had been quite early when she had left the comfort and warmth of her bed. At least they had beaten the heat of the day, however, and now she was glad to be sitting as the noon sun beat mercilessly down.

The prophets of Baal had been appealing to their obviously disinterested god the whole of the day, and Rachel had long grown weary of watching their antics. The more she watched the faces of the prophets, the more convinced she was about their similarity to Elihu's face. As the reality of it settled in her mind, the humor of it left her to be replaced by fear and depression. This was to be her life, at the side of one such as these, whose eyes held no joy, no humor, but something much darker.

Rachel shuddered. She shut her own eyes trying to block out the image and sat down. At least she was alone now. She had told her father that she needed to stretch her legs and had excused herself. Now here she sat at the very edge of the circle of people, unable to bring herself to return. She looked up into the cloudless sky. Would it ever rain again?

Her mind flew to one particularly rainy afternoon long ago, before her mother had died. The rain had poured steadily all day, and as a child of about four years, this had dismayed Rachel who had been forced to sit inside the house all day long. Her mother had noticed her daughter's frustration with the weather and had stopped her work long enough to tell her of a time when there had been no rain for seven years:

"People wanted rain very badly, but none came. There was no rain to water the plants, so no food could grow," her mother had explained, setting Rachel on her lap.

"Did the people all die?" Rachel had inquired with wide eyes.

"No, the people did not die because God took care of them. He had already told someone a long time before that there would be seven years without rain, so that he could tell the king, and the people could store up food for when the time came."

"Hey! That was Joseph!" Rachel had gleefully announced, clapping her hands at her remembrance of the story of the boy whose brothers threw him into a pit and sold him to Egypt.

Her mother had laughed at her daughter's enthusiasm. "Yes, dear, it was Joseph. God knew even when Joseph was a little boy that someday there would be no rain for a long, long time, and that Joseph would save the people by having them store up food. God is always looking out for us. Even when do not know it."

Unaware that her cheeks were wet with tears, Rachel smiled at the recollection of her beautiful mother holding her tightly in her arms as she told her of God's care for her. She had always told Rachel that no matter what happened, God was looking out for his beautiful little girl.

But there was no one here now to tell her this. It had not rained for three years, and she was going to be married to an awful man, and there was no one to tell her that God would make it all right.

Rachel shook her head. "I just don't see how this could ever be made all right," she whispered.

At that moment, a great commotion behind her forced Rachel back to the situation at hand. She turned to see that something had once again caught the attention of the crowd. She ran back, standing on tiptoe to see what was happening.

It was Elijah. He was calling to everyone to come closer to him.

Rachel managed somehow to find her father again and stood beside him as she watched in anticipation.

Elijah was repairing the altar of the Lord.

~

It had been a very long time since this particular altar had served to honor God with its offering. Athalia observed Hannah's reverent look as this prophet began to restore it.

Elijah had taken twelve large stones to rebuild it. Hannah had explained to Athalia earlier that these symbolized the twelve tribes of Israel. Now he was digging a deep trench around it.

There was a general murmur as the people looking on wondered about the curious actions of Elijah. Athalia voiced the confusion aloud. "Why would he dig a trench?" She had seen many sacrifices before, but this was a first. Of what possible use would a trench be?

She looked over to see Hannah just shrug and smile. What a strange girl. She was obviously unable to explain the action, but still seemed to trust this man of God impeccably. Her smile seemed to say, "Whatever the reason, it is a good one."

Athalia was not so certain, but she held her tongue and turned back to Elijah who was now preparing the bull. She watched as the familiar procedure of cutting the bull and laying the pieces on the altar took place.

She glanced down, suddenly aware that her hands were clenched tightly at her sides. She was getting nervous. This whole day up to this point had been spent watching the prophets of the god with whom she was so familiar generally make a fool of themselves. She knew the customs and traditions of Baal worship inside and out. She had spent her life watching such rituals daily. She also knew the extent to which they seemed to gain Baal's attention. Never had Athalia witnessed anything that would indicate that Baal gave any mind to those so intent on serving him. Today had been no different. This came as no surprise to Athalia. She had concluded long ago that if there was a Baal, he did not care about humans no matter how much they tried to appease him.

Now here was this single prophet of another god, who claimed that his was the one true God. This was one prophet who dared to stand alone and defy the god to whom she had been taught reverence. It was not this fact that bothered Athalia, for she had grown to hate the very name of Baal. But what of this prophet named Elijah? She had to admire his courage at any rate. And what of this strange girl standing next to her who seemed so confident that Elijah was right? These were two people she had come to admire greatly in such a very short time. As a matter of fact, when Athalia thought about it, these were the only two people she could ever remember admiring at all.

Suddenly it became very important to her that they were right. She could not stand the thought that they might have been deceived into believing something that was not real.

Athalia looked again at Hannah's smiling face, eyes sparkling with excitement. She just hoped Hannah would not be too disappointed.

She looked back at Elijah and gave a gasp. "What is he doing now? Is that water they are pouring over it?"

It was. Some of the prophets of Baal who had not fainted from loss of blood or exhaustion were filling four barrels full of water and pouring them over the altar at the request of Elijah himself. Athalia shook her head slowly, mouth agape as she stared at the men filling and dumping the barrels three times and then proceeding to fill the trench to the top with water.

She looked back at Hannah. Surely now she could not possibly believe that this soaked altar even had the potential to burn! But, to her amazement, she found the face unaltered, smiling with confidence at the scene before them.

Curiously, Athalia found herself relieved at the lack of concern her new friend seemed to have. "You really believe he is going to do it, don't you? Your God, I mean."

Hannah looked over and her smile widened. "There is nothing else I can believe."

Athalia thought for a moment about that statement. Athalia had spent her life observing the worship and actions of Baal. She knew what to expect from him based on her own experience, and it was therefore no surprise to see that he did not respond today.

This girl beside her had spent her life worshipping and observing the actions of her God. Had her experience with her God been different than Athalia's? Did she have different expectations based on experience?

Athalia found herself hoping with all that was in her that her friend was not to be disappointed.

A hush fell over the hill as Elijah raised his voice toward heaven. "LORD God of Abraham, Isaac, and Israel, let it be known this day that You are God in Israel and I am Your servant, and that I have done all these things at Your word."[5]

"At your word?" Athalia repeated with confusion. "Does God actually speak to this man?"

"Hear me, O LORD," Elijah continued, "hear me, that this people may know that You are the LORD God, and that You have turned their hearts back to You again."[6]

Then she saw it happen. The fire came. Falling from somewhere unseen, the fire landed on the altar. Athalia squinted her eyes to see through the smoke. Everything was gone. All was consumed by the fire: the bull, the wood, the stones, the dust. Even the water had been consumed.

Athalia was unaware of the people around her falling to their faces. She did not hear the almost uniform cry of "The Lord! He is God!" which went up around her. She did not hear Elijah's call to capture the prophets of Baal, nor did she notice the commotion as the men ran after them. She did not see Hannah kneel beside her, the smile still in place with hands raised in silent adoration. She was oblivious even to her own sobs shaking her small frame or the tears streaming down her cheeks.

Athalia was unaware of everything except the fire. She could not tear her gaze from the place where the blaze had so suddenly fallen and consumed. It was a mere spark now, licking the last few drops of water from the trench, yet Athalia saw the flames as clearly as she had moments before.

5. 1 Kings 18:36b (NKJV)
6. 1 Kings 18:37 (NKJV)

Elijah was right. His God really was the one true God. Not only was this a powerful God who could send fire that would consume even water, but he did so in response to a request. He was paying attention. This God was neither asleep nor on vacation. This God was not too busy to listen to his servant, and even, it sounded like, to talk to him and give him directions.

Athalia fell to her knees as the realization hit her as clearly and suddenly as the fire which had dropped from heaven. The God of Israel was real and bigger that she could have possibly imagined. She suddenly felt little. So very little.

And so very evil. "Oh, God, what do I do now?"

All she could do was sob.

~

Hannah rose from her knees and looked up at the afternoon sky. Was it really just last evening that she had been watching the sky and yelling at the very same God who had just dropped fire from heaven to consume water, rock, and sacrifice?

Hannah shuddered. She had always known God to be powerful; she had heard and believed all the amazing stories of how he had performed wonder after wonder for the Israelites, everything from parting a sea to sending food from heaven every day for forty years. She had never doubted the truth of these stories, and yet today something had shifted in her perception. Today she had witnessed a display of his greatness that could never be erased from her memory.

And it unnerved her. Her God was good. He was gracious. He was merciful. But today, she realized in a new way that he was not to be messed with. All creation was at his command.

"It is such a good thing for us that he is so merciful," she whispered as she looked around for Athalia.

~

Micah dragged his exhausted body back up the hill to look for Hannah one more time before he left for home. His father had long since taken Nathaniel and left, claiming that the small boy was too young to watch the slaughter, even if it was that of the prophets of such a vile deity as Baal.

Micah had been one of the slayers. When Elijah had made the call for the capture of the prophets of Baal, Micah was one of the first to rise from his face and take off after them. He had been waiting his whole life for an opportunity to help destroy the evil that had infiltrated Israel in the form of false gods and did not hesitate when the opportunity presented itself. Now they were gone. The four hundred plus men who had spent the day crying in vain to their silent god were now lying silent themselves by the brook, and Micah was headed back up the hill to make one final search for his sister before returning home.

"Micah!"

He spun around at the sound of his name.

"I'm so glad you found us!" Hannah smiled. "I was beginning to worry about our returning alone."

"Us?" Micah raised an eyebrow.

"Athalia and I . . . Oh! I forgot! You do not know her!" Hannah laughed softly. "It feels as though I have known her for so much longer than just this day." She turned and motioned to the prostrate form a few yards away. "She is Athalia. She is the one I saw by the tree this morning when I left you and Father. I really do not think she is well. She has not said, but I think she hasn't any place to stay. She must come home with us. She has been in that same position since soon after the fire fell, but we must convince her to come with us."

Micah smiled and shook his head as he watched his sister go to the stranger and lean down to invite her home with them. She had found someone to pour her ever flowing mercy into. "Maybe this will keep her mind off of her fears for Samuel," he thought to himself.

～

"No! I couldn't!" Athalia shook her head at the suggestion. To think of one such as herself, a temple prostitute, going home with one such as Hannah! It was absurd!

"Where will you go then?" Hannah inquired softly.

Athalia dropped her eyes, unable to answer.

"Please at least come home with us for this night. If you decide, after a night, that you cannot stay, then at least you will be rested for whatever comes next."

Athalia glanced down at her belly. "Whatever comes next." What did come next? What was the plan? She had successfully removed her child from the evil of the temple, but now what? Somehow, she knew that she must do everything in her power to keep her child alive and tell him about this true God whose power she had just witnessed. Well, this was one night, at least, she could keep him safe. Raising her eyes to meet the smiling ones of this strange girl, she nodded her head, and rose to her feet.

4

"They sing the song of Moses, the servant of God, and the song of
the Lamb, saying: 'Great and marvelous are Your works, Lord God
Almighty! Just and true are Your ways, O King of the saints!'"

REVELATION 15:3 (NKJV)

"Oh Nathaniel! You do brighten up a room!"

Nathaniel frowned as he watched his mother wipe a tear from
the corner of her eye which was crinkled in laughter. "I don't see
what is so funny about it! Shalom could have been burned by the
fire if I hadn't put him in my cloak!"

"I just cannot believe you managed to keep him hidden until
you had traveled too far for your father to turn back to take him
back home! I'm so sorry I missed his expression when he noticed
that lamb . . ." Her sentence was choked out by another giggle.
Then, more seriously she added, "Nathaniel, you know you are getting too attached to that lamb."

"I know it has to go back to the flock soon, but Micah said I
can start going with him to help with the sheep. You know I will
take Micah's job as the shepherd in a few years. He said it is about
time I start learning how. Then I will get to see Shalom all the time!
I will get to see him grow up!"

"Nathaniel . . ." The lines of laughter faded from her face as
her voice trailed off searching for words.

When no words came, the boy knelt by the mat. "Are you ok Mama? Do you hurt? Mama, when are you going to be better?"

"I do not know, Nathaniel. I am not sure I will get better," Miriam replied as she drew him closer to her.

Nathaniel glared down into the tiny face of the suckling infant at his mother's breast as he felt his mother's arm pulling him even closer to her.

"Nathaniel, little Abbigail needs you. She is going to need a big brother to look out for her. See how tiny she is?"

Nathaniel continued to stare silently.

"It is not her fault, Nathaniel. I was not well long before I had her. Her birth just added a bit of a strain. That's all."

One small tear squeezed from Nathaniel's eyelid as he lay his head down on his mother's shoulder, gaze still locked onto the wriggling infant.

Mariam softly patted the small head resting against her. After a moment she said, "Is that your sister I hear? They must be back."

"I will go see," he said swiping the tear away and scrambling from the bed and out of the room.

Moments later the child came bursting back into the room.

"Mama! Hannah brought a friend home! Isn't she pretty?"

Miriam smiled as Hannah and the "friend" entered the room behind the boy. The girl, she noticed at a glance stood straight and tall, with downcast eyes and trembling hands clasped together in front of her. "Yes, Nathaniel, she is beautiful." Then, turning towards her daughter she inquired, "Who, might I ask, is this beautiful girl you have brought to me?"

"This is Athalia, mother. I found her looking quite ill on our way to Mount Carmel and . . ."

"Hello dear," Miriam cut her daughter off, holding out a hand and a smile to the girl. "It is so good to have a guest in the house again. We do not have much opportunity for entertaining guests anymore."

"Thank you for allowing me in your home, ma'am," Athalia replied lifting her eyes slowly to the kind voice of welcome. When her gaze met that of the welcomer, she let out a deep breath. More smiling eyes.

"Any friend of Hannah's is welcome, child."

∼

The sun was low in the sky, but its intensity was still great, and Hannah had chosen the roof for the slight breeze it offered as the perfect place to pick clean a wad of wool and then comb it to prepare for spinning. She could hear snatches of gossiping villagers who passed by and was glad to be up where they would not expect her to enter into the conversations. The talk this evening revolved exclusively around the amazing events of the day which had taken place atop Mount Carmel.

"I wonder what that high and mighty Queen Jezebel is thinking now that all of her precious prophets have been killed?"

"Oooo . . . I would not want to be Elijah when she finds out!"

"Serves her right, bringing in her nasty old idols into Samaria . . ."

Hannah sighed. She recognized the voices as those of women who had been quick themselves to bow down to Jezebel's gods when she had become queen a few years before. It was only a very few who had remained loyal to the God of Israel. Hannah was grateful for her own father who had refused to have anything to do with the false gods and had continued to make the trek to Jerusalem every year to offer a sacrifice for his family. He had taught his children reverence for the one true God alone. Maybe today's events would change the hearts of others in Israel who had not been so loyal. One could hope.

As Hannah bent down to pick up a comb, a dark head popped up over the side of the thatch roof.

"Who is the girl with Nathaniel?" Rachel's cheerful voice inquired.

Hannah did not even look up. "Athalia. Her name is Athalia."

Rachel cocked her head thoughtfully before climbing up over the ladder onto the roof. "That does not sound Hebrew. How do you know her?"

"I saw her this morning on my way to Mount Carmel, and she was not doing too well, so I brought her home. I don't think she has anywhere else to go."

Rachel shrugged as she plopped down on the packed earth beside her friend.

"Hannah, do you really think that God is watching all the time? That he is looking out for us? Not just for the whole nation, but for you? And for me?"

Hannah set the wool down and turned to her friend. "What is it that you would like for me to say? You have heard the same stories as I."

Rachel sighed and drew patterns in the dirt with a twig. "I know. But it is just so hard to trust it."

"Trust what? That God cares about you?"

"That he will make it all right."

"This is about Elihu." Hannah's brow wrinkled as she put a hand on the bowed shoulder by her side.

Rachel nodded silently. Slowly she turned to look at her friend. "Hannah, I know you keep saying it, but do you really believe it will all be well even though you haven't heard anything about Samuel in over a week?"

Hannah looked up into the sky as if the answer could be found in the depth of the blue. Did she believe all would be well?

She heard the soft bleating of the lamb below in the courtyard. Shalom. It is well. What did that really mean?

Was it only well if things went according to her own plans and desires? Hannah knew, or thought she knew anyway, that she trusted the God who had created everything. But trust him to do what? Trust him to make things the way she wanted them to be? Or just plain trusted him to be God, good and holy in all he did and allowed? She had her own definite idea as to what would be good in her own situation, her own life with Samuel, but what if God thought differently? What if Samuel never came back? What if something awful had happened to him? Would that mean all was not well? Would that affect her own idea about God's goodness?

What was it that her father had quoted a few nights ago from the writings of Job? "Though He slay me, yet will I trust Him."[1]

Hannah let her gaze drift back to Rachel. "I just don't know anymore. I think . . . I think it has to be well. If God is really as we have been told, if he really is concerned for his creation, if he cares at all, then it must all be well for each of us, because he is in charge of it all, even if it does not match up to our own ideas about what is well. If not, there really isn't much use to believing any of it, is there?"

Rachel pondered the words carefully for a moment before saying, "Hannah, I really believe there is something evil about Elihu. I am scared to spend the rest of my life as his wife."

Hannah placed her hand on the shaking knee of her friend.

After a moment of sitting silently, staring down at her friend's hand on her knee, Rachel suddenly cocked her head. "Did a shadow just pass over us?" she inquired looking up.

She gasped and Hannah followed her gaze skyward. A shadow *had* passed over them. The shadow of a large, looming, dark cloud. The two girls stared with wide eyes as the cloud slowly consumed the sky. A strong wind began to whip at their hair until it was pulled from the braids that held it, and neither could see without holding it behind them at their necks.

Holding their free hands out, the girls watched as tiny drops of water appeared in their palms.

Rachel threw her arms around Hannah's neck. "It's raining!" she cried. "After three years, it's raining!"

Suddenly Rachel pulled back and looked at her friend with a smile. "All is well."

∼

Micah watched from the doorway as the rain fell in great sheets on the two dancing figures out in the street. Nathaniel had known it would not take much persuading to talk Rachel into playing with him in the rain, so there they were, singing and jumping around in the downpour. Nathaniel was shaking a tambourine as Rachel danced around him, her hands holding the bottom of her

---

1. Job 13:15 (NKJV)

tunic up out of the puddles as she sang. Micah could make out the words of a song an ancient king had written long ago:

> "Oh, clap your hands, all you peoples!
> Shout to God with the voice of triumph!
> For the LORD Most High is awesome;
> He is a great King over all the earth."[2]

A month ago, Micah would have been out there with them, but not today.

"Come on Micah! You won't melt!" Rachel had laughed trying to pull him out the door with them, but he had quietly refused claiming that he was too old for such silliness. Rachel had winced at the jab, and stared for a moment in confusion, but then quickly disappeared out the door after Nathaniel.

Now he stood under the slight shelter of the courtyard entry, watching them, sorry that he had let the bitter words escape. A soft hand rested on his arm, and he looked over to see his sister's concerned look.

"It hurts you that she is getting married."

When there was no response, Hannah continued, "You know, you really hurt her by your words and actions lately. Love is not selfish, Micah. If you love her only so that she will love you back, is that really love?"

Micah turned back to look at the two dancing in the rain. Rachel's laughing form had Nathaniel by the arms as she spun him around. He knew Hannah was right and hated that he knew it. It was just so much easier to be bitter and angry. So much less painful.

After a moment, he felt Hannah squeeze his arm slightly, and then brush past him out the door, hands held high.

Micah stood watching the much-desired water fall in great sheets onto the dancing trio. He stood listening to the sound of the tambourine and the melody of thankful voices blending with the rush of the wind and rain. He stood feeling the spray of the water droplets that were blowing into the courtyard entrance.

And at long last, he stopped standing, and stepped out to join in the celebration.

2. Psalm 47:1,2 (NKJV)

5

"Now when he had taken the scroll, the four living creatures and the twenty-four elders fell down before the Lamb, each having a harp, and golden bowls full of incense, which are the prayers of the saints."

REVELATION 5:8 (NKJV)

DAVID SAT OUTSIDE THE mud dwelling watching the raindrops hit the puddle at his feet. His knees were drawn up to his chest, his arms holding them tightly together. The drops were coming more slowly now, and he watched as each one plopped into the small pool creating a ring that spread out slowly to meet and connect with the other rings made by the other droplets. He hardly noticed that the drops were also falling onto his own head, sliding down strands of his hair and dropping into the puddle to meet up with the ones directly from the heavens.

He had thought he would feel differently when the rains finally came again. Joy? Peace? Relief?

But it was none of those emotions that filled the space of his heart as he sat there staring at the much longed for water at his feet.

What did it really matter anyway? The rain could not bring his father back. And now there was this new situation in which he found himself that had brought with it a whole other set of stinging emotions.

"In which he found himself." David scoffed at his own mind's terminology. "In which he had placed himself" would be more accurate. His father would have known what to do. There had never been a scrap he had gotten himself into as a child that his father had not known how to remedy with exactly the right words.

But his father could not help him now.

David squeezed his eyes closed against the memory of that horrible day last year, but no matter how tightly he tried to shut it out, his mind's eye saw clearly his mother's sobbing form kneeling in the dust as his father was led away in chains by Jezebel's army.

"If Father's god really is the one true God, why is it that the prophets of Baal are alive and thriving and the prophets of the one true God were all slaughtered at the orders of Queen Jezebel?" David muttered toward the puddle.

Well, almost all. There was Elijah who had managed somehow to escape the sword of Jezebel. But he was such a strange man. David had even heard a rumor that Elijah was the reason there had been no rain for so long, that he had even told King Ahab that there would be no rain until he said so.

"You have to think bigger, David," his father had said when he had asked him about the rumor. "Life is so much bigger than just us and what we can see. God's plans are big, and we are just little parts of them. We have to trust that when things he does look strange to us, and even inconvenient or painful, he has something bigger in mind and those things are a necessary part of the plan."

When David had shaken his head at that answer his father had placed a hand on David's shoulder and continued, looking straight into David's eyes. "But he is good, David. Always good. And that means we can trust it is all really for our good."

But the price was high for believing, and David questioned the goodness of a God who would allow his father to pay such a price. And so, he had not gone when Elijah had called for all of Israel to gather at Mount Carmel a few days before. He had no interest in what Elijah had to say.

David lowered his chin to his knees and sighed. Listening to the steady drops of rain still falling, he wondered if the rumors had been true. Maybe that was why Elijah had called all the people to the mountain. Maybe he had decided to ask God for rain again.

～

Inside the hut, the man strained to pull himself out of the darkness, as slowly the veil of fog about his eyes began to clear. The first sight that his eyes could pull into focus was the sleeping form of an older woman, legs outstretched, sitting on the floor beside him. Her head was back against the mud wall. Her hands, which were lying limply on each side of her held wet rags.

Wondering where he was and how he had gotten there, the man tried to rise, but found he had no strength. With great effort, he turned his head to look about him, fighting the wave of nausea that swept over him. He was lying on a mat which he saw took up about a quarter of the entire floor space of the mud shelter. Two clay pots and a few cooking utensils were all that occupied the small abode other than himself and the sleeping form beside him. A small amount of light was seeping through the cracks of the door directly across from him, so he knew it must be day. "What day?" he wondered.

The woman stirred, and the confused man waited. Maybe this woman could set in order all the random thoughts and questions floating through his still quite groggy head.

"Praise the Lord."

The whispered words drew his attention to the smiling face of the woman who had awaken. "Such a peaceful face," he thought as she leaned over him to wipe his brow with the wet rag in her hand.

"I was beginning to lose hope, but here you are, awake, and the fever seems to have broken."

"How long have I been here?" he asked startled by the weakness of his own voice.

"A little over a week."

Over a week! He closed his eyes trying to remember what events had brought him here. Suddenly his eyes flew open to look up at the kind face hovering over him. "The bracelet!" he croaked out. "Where is the bracelet?"

The woman sat back on her heels, and her gaze filled with concern. "You don't remember, do you? You were brought here by my son who found you lying unconscious by the side of the road. You had been beaten badly so we assumed you had been robbed and left for dead. There was no money or anything of value with you when we found you."

The woman stood to her feet. "You need rest. I will leave you to it."

He squinted momentarily as the daylight flooded in with the opening of the door and then was quickly shut out again, but not before he had caught a sweet scent that sparked his memory. He lay back and smiled as his ears became focused on the soft patter above him. It was as though some small animal was dancing on the roof.

"Rain. Finally. Rain," he whispered as his body drifted into sleep to the soft lullaby dropping from heaven.

∼

"He is awake."

David looked up from the puddle to the gentle face of his mother. "Really? Good. That's good," he said turning back to the puddle and nodding his head slowly as the news settled in.

"Yes, it certainly is," Jerusha said squatting down beside him and arranging her tunic in a vain attempt to keep it off the wet ground. "He is resting now."

David nodded again.

"You are troubled."

David looked over at his mother and smiled weakly. "No, mother. I am fine. I am glad he is doing well."

"But you are troubled none the less. The rains have come, the man we have nursed day and night for the past week is awake, and yet, you are troubled."

David sat silently for a few moments pulling a stick through the puddle.

"Mother, how is it that you are not troubled? How is it that you are always so peaceful and . . . and . . . not troubled!" He threw the stick from him.

Jerusha set a gentle hand on her son's knee. "You know I trust the Lord to take care of us. I need not trouble myself about it."

David turned towards his mother. "You watched as your husband was led away to be killed. He was killed because he served the very Lord you say takes care of us. How can you still believe he is good?"

Jerusha winced, and her eyes filled with tears at the memory, but she continued to look directly into the troubled gaze of her son. "You know the stories of the children of Israel coming into the promised land, right?"

David nodded. Of course, he did. How could he not? It was his father's favorite past time to recount the many adventures of God's people. Many a night he had fallen asleep to the animated voice of his father telling how God had saved his people time and time again.

His mother continued, "For every story of a victorious battle, there were mothers and sons who lost husbands and fathers. The battles were won, often in amazing, glorious ways, but there were still almost always some lost in the battle. That means that even in victory, there were those who grieved. I don't know when I will be able to see that the big battle is won, but I believe that your father's death was just a part of the big victory. I choose to believe God sees the victory."

David dropped his gaze. "You have to think bigger," he murmured as the words echoed in his memory.

"What was that?" Jerusha asked.

"Nothing." David shook his head. "I just can't see how you can be so sure."

"I choose to be sure. I think that at some point we all have to choose to be sure of something, or life will not hold any sort of peace or enjoyment at all. All my life I have heard the stories of God's care for his people. Given the evidence of those and my own personal experience of his care, I chose long ago to put my trust in the God of your father. When your father died, I had to choose all over again in a sense. It had cost him dearly to choose the Lord, and suddenly I had to decide if I was willing to trust a God who allowed such searing pain to touch my life."

"And you decided it was good of God to do that?"

"I looked at my options. I could decide to put my trust in other gods . . ." She laughed. "And there were certainly plenty to choose from around here!" Then her face grew serious again. "But that didn't take long to rule out. I have seen what serving those gods produces, and it is certainly not joy or peace. Or I could continue to trust a God who has faithfully led his people this far and leave to him to decide whether my part of his plan, his good plan, involves pain or not."

David rose to his feet. "Or you could have chosen to not trust any god at all. You could have chosen to realize that you just have to work hard and figure things out for yourself, because there may not be any powerful beings looking out for us!"

Jerusha looked up at her son who was now pacing in front of her. "Yes. Yes, I could have chosen that option. But that road looks dark and hopeless. And I choose hope."

~

"So, you are the one who found me. Thank you."

David dropped his gaze to the dirt floor.

Jerusha knelt down by the mat. "So now that you are awake and seem a bit more lucid, can you tell us about yourself? Is there anyone you want to send a message to? Anyone who may be worried about you?"

"Yes," came the strained answer. "Hannah. Get a message to Hannah."

6

"For the Lamb who is in the midst of the throne will shepherd them
and lead them to living fountains of water. And God will wipe away
every tear from their eyes."

REVELATION 7:17 (NKJV)

A FAST MELODY WAS flowing out from the olive grove this morning where Athalia sat. She had taught herself to play the tiny flute
as soon as she had been old enough to figure out how it worked.
Somehow, the music had always seemed to drive away the oppressive darkness that had so frightened her at nights in the temple.

Now she played to drive away a different fear.

Her mind's eye could still see the fire falling. Her fingers flew
over the tiny holes in the flute desperate to erase the image of the
fire licking up the water and melting the rocks. Who had ever
heard of fire that could consume water and stone? And summoned
at the request of a man to his god?

That was something. Something to consider with a great
amount of respect. There was a real being, an enormously powerful being, who had answered Elijah.

What must this being think of her?

Breathless, Athalia set down her flute and looked up, scan-
ning the sky trying to imagine just where that fire had come from.
Was he looking down now? Could he see her under that tree?

Athalia shivered and lowered her gaze to the ground. It was best not to draw too much attention to herself. A God who would send fire to consume water and stones after his servant had just implored the people to stop serving Baal would certainly have no use for one who had allowed her body to be given to the worship of that very God.

But maybe, just maybe the child had a chance, she thought as she glanced down at her belly. He had not made any bad choices yet. He had yet to make any choices at all. Maybe if she could somehow keep him connected to this family . . .

Athalia felt certain that this God of fire was pleased with Hannah and her family. This was the thought that had kept her here these last few days.

"Please stay," Hannah had implored just that very morning. "We all love having you and Nathaniel would be heartbroken if you left!"

Athalia smiled at the image of Nathaniel's tiny face staring up into her own in adoration. Now, as she sat watching the colors of the sun beams dance on drops of water that were clinging to blades of grass, she made her decision.

Yes, for the child, she would stay.

Then, leaning her head back against the tree and closing her eyes, Athalia thought through the story she would have to tell as her swelling belly became more and more evident. The truth was not an option, of course. But what could she say to explain the baby? Maybe that she was a widow. Yes. That might work. She was recent widow whose husband had starved to death because of the famine. That seemed plausible. And then, having no family nearby, she had decided to set out on her own to find work.

Athalia shrugged. It wasn't the greatest story, but maybe they would not ask any more questions. Then, when the child was born safely in their home, she would leave. She knew that she did not belong in such a family, but she also knew they would raise her child to know and serve the God she had seen answer a man.

Athalia opened her eyes and looked down at her belly and rubbed it lovingly. "I love you little guy. I love you so much, and

I want you in the favor of that powerful God who sent fire from heaven. Who knows? Maybe he will even listen to you when you are older? Maybe he will answer your requests like he did Elijah."

She lay her head back against the tree again as the tears began to fall with her resolve. She swallowed the lump in her throat. When it came to it, how would she ever find the courage to leave this child?

As the tears continued to fall, Athalia picked up the tiny flute and began to play again.

~

David sat down by the side of the road to catch his breath. He knew he should be nearing his destination according to Samuel's directions, but the rapid pace which he had kept throughout the morning and part of the afternoon had left him exhausted, and he needed to rest before facing the one to whom he carried the good news.

Good news. David gave a short, bitter laugh. Yes, he was sure the girl would think it wonderful news. She would likely be ever so grateful to him for the message.

Of course, if she were ever to know the truth, she would not be nearly so pleased with the messenger. David shivered at the recollection of what had transpired that evening by the road.

A sweet sound interrupted the bitter musing. David caught his breath. A lovely tune seemed to drip down around him like the rain that had come days before to the dry thirsty land. An old memory was stirred, and he swung around half expecting to see a flock of sheep. He glanced around. No sheep. Just a small grove of olive trees. Rising, he was pulled towards the enchanting melody that grew louder and clearer as he approached.

Then he saw her. She sat with her head resting back against a tree, her dark hair in one long twist tossed over one shoulder. Her eyes were closed, and one bright tear clung to the dark lashes. The bamboo flute from which the delicious sound sprang was raised to her lips.

David stepped back for fear he would startle the beautiful girl and the music would stop. Closing his eyes, David let the sound envelope his heart, seeping into his soul and feeling as if it were pushing out the guilt and bitterness that had taken up residence there.

He wondered if this was what King Saul must have felt all those years ago when the shepherd boy would play his harp for him:

"Then Saul would become refreshed and well, and the distressing spirit would depart from him,"[1] his dad had recounted to him.

Refreshed. Well. Like a distressing spirit had lifted from his heart. Yes, David could relate.

But then it stopped. David opened his eyes to see the flute drop to the ground as the girl jumped to her feet.

"Oh," she cried covering her mouth with both hands, "I did not know anyone was there!"

"Please, I am so sorry to have startled you. The music was . . . it was beautiful. Are you a shepherdess?"

The girl cocked her head. "Shepherdess?"

"I just thought . . . I mean I heard the shepherd's flute . . ." David bent to pick up the reed pipe.

The girl's eyes widened as she slowly took the flute from his hand.

"I am sorry, I was just passing by . . ." David stumbled over his words. "I have a message for someone in the village. Someone named Hannah. Do you know her?"

The girl, still staring at the flute in her hand, nodded, and, without looking up, turned towards the village, and David followed.

Athalia stood silently, bouncing baby Abbigail on her hip as she stared towards the doorway from which Hannah had just exited. She had been told about the missing Samuel and wondered if the stranger's news was of him. She hoped with all her heart that if it was, it was good news.

1. 1 Samuel 16:23b (NKJV)

"What a man he must be to win the heart of someone like Hannah," she whispered softly to herself.

Abbigail gave a happy little squeal drawing Athalia's attention from the doorway to the tiny life in her arms. Athalia laughed and looked down into the smiling face of the baby.

"You agree, don't you? Your sister is someone pretty special. She deserves to be happy. I bet your God would do that for her."

Abbigail reached out and grabbed hold of Athalia's finger. "Look at you," Athalia whispered. "so tiny, so perfect, so innocent."

Athalia's eyes filled with tears. "Oh, to be innocent again. To have the God of Israel smile down on me as he surely does on you and your family."

She leaned forward and kissed the delicate fingers wrapped tightly around her own.

"Do you have any idea how blessed you are little one?" she asked as she laid the tiny child on a wool rug that was lying on the floor of the courtyard and turned to the clay oven to finish the bread Hannah had been baking when Athalia had arrived with the stranger.

She pulled off a chunk of the dough Hannah had kneaded and patted it into a flat circle as she watched the infant kick her tiny feet and punch her fists into the air. She glanced over at the wooden instrument lying next to the wriggling infant. A shepherd's flute, the stranger had called it. Had one or both of her parents been shepherds?

She slapped the flattened circle of dough onto the interior wall of the cylindrical clay oven and pulled off another chunk of dough.

Shepherds. Having been raised in the temple, she was not very familiar with the profession. She had noted that Hannah's brother tended sheep. Why had neither he nor Hannah ever mentioned the flute?

Another piece of dough was collected. Pulling. Patting. Slapping. Wondering.

With the final piece of dough formed and slapped to the inside of the oven, Athalia sighed. Well, at least she had another piece to add to the story she would tell . . . a poor widowed mother to be whose husband had been a shepherd . . .

~

Nathaniel skipped happily beside the long pace of his father. How long he had waited to get to participate in the harvest! He was too little to handle the sickles, but he would get to watch and bring water out to the thirsty men who swung the heavy iron blades. He realized there would not be much barley to harvest, but the endless vessels of water that had been carried to the thirsty fields over the winter had kept enough of it alive for the latter rains that had finally come to have something to water. Nathaniel could hardly wait! First Elijah and now this!

"That was our God who made that fire come down, wasn't it, Daddy?"

"Yes, it was, Nathaniel." Joseph smiled down into the up-turned face of the boy whose hand grasped tightly to his own. "It certainly was."

Nathaniel's gaze dropped to the rocky ground on which they were walking this warm afternoon. His eyebrows pushed together, and he chewed on his tongue. After a few moments of silence, Nathaniel raised his face again to his father's.

"If our God can make fire come down whenever he wants, why aren't people more afraid of him?"

Joseph looked down into the serious little face once more. "That, my son, is a very good question. Why do you think it might be?"

Nathaniel cocked his head and pressed his lips together. "I guess 'cause he doesn't do it very often."

Nathaniel's gaze dropped once again to the pebbles beneath his feet. Then he sighed deeply. "If I was God, I'd drop fire down whenever somebody did something bad."

"Hmmm." Joseph squeezed the little hand in his own and raised his gaze to the fluffy clouds floating above. "It seems to me if he were to do that there wouldn't be anyone left."

"No Daddy." Nathaniel stopped walking and pulled on his arm. "Only the bad people would be gone."

Joseph stooped down until he was at eye level with his son and met his serious gaze. "Nathaniel, you tell me, if God dropped fire down every time someone did something bad, who would be left?"

"We would . . . wouldn't we?" The certainty was fading from the big brown eyes.

"You have never done anything that God didn't like?"

Nathaniel's eyes dropped remembering how mad he was at baby Abbigail this morning, and how he had made a face at her when his mother wasn't looking. He remembered how he had wished she had never been born. God probably did not like that too much. Slowly he raised his face back to his father's.

"I guess it's a good thing for me God doesn't send fire every time."

Joseph patted the small head and smiled. "It's a good thing for all of us, Nathaniel."

～

Samuel watched as a young woman passed quickly by, an empty basket on her head. It was sure to be full when she returned later, probably with fruit, Samuel thought as he sat outside the small hut for the first time since his arrival. The village was not unlike his own, he noted, yet on a much smaller scale, and poorer. Based on the traffic he observed, each small hut lining the street must contain anywhere from five to ten residents. The widow and her son seemed to be the exception.

He looked down the street and saw an older woman kneeling outside her own little home, pressing grain in a stone mortar with a pestle. The cooking here appeared to be done out of doors, with small clay ovens set up outside every door.

On a nearby rooftop another woman sat busily weaving on a loom.

Looking out towards the fields where he was sure most of the men of the village were already busy at work, Samuel sighed. If life had gone as he had planned, he too would be out in the fields of his own village right now. And Hannah would be his wife.

Samuel thought back to about this time last year when he had met with her father and arranged the betrothal. His own father had owned the field adjacent to Hannah's, and so the two were well acquainted. Since his father's death, Hannah's father had taken it upon himself to see to it that Samuel was well provided for and had eventually come to think of him as a son, so it had come as neither a surprise, nor a problem when Samuel had finally asked for his daughter's hand in marriage. It was decided that it would benefit both parties to combine their land and flocks once the two were married. Then Samuel and Joseph would work the land together while Hannah continued to help her sick mother with the smaller children. He would also be able to trade off the shepherding of the small flocks with Micah until the economy improved allowing them to hire shepherds again.

It seemed the perfect arrangement. Samuel had spent the last year preparing the house for them, working the land, and taking his turn tending the sheep. He had not gone to see Hannah since the betrothal, as was the custom, though it had been hard to avoid her, especially as he was working closely with both her father and brother.

And he missed her face.

As a child, he had been practically raised at her side as his own mother had died in childbirth, and his father was such good friends with Joseph. He even remembered Hannah's own birth, though vaguely as he had been only six years old at the time.

But he remembered quite clearly the day he realized that she was no longer a baby.

It was the day his father had died. Samuel had found him out in the field, and, not knowing what to do, had run straight to find Joseph. It was Hannah he had seen first, however, and blurted out, "He's dead! Get your father! I need help!"

It was then that he noticed for the first time her face. It was beautiful. So peaceful. So gentle and full of light and yet filling with grief for his own pain as his words penetrated. For a moment all he could do was to gaze back into those eyes and hold onto the peace that they held which somehow eased his own aching heart.

It was not until several weeks later, after all the funeral ceremonies had ended and life had settled into a dull and lonelier existence that Samuel remembered that face and the peace it had brought to him that horrible day. It was then he had decided he wanted that face to be a part of his life forever.

Just over a week ago he had sent word to her to be ready, for he would soon arrive to take her as his wife. Then he had set his feet towards the city to have a stone that had once belonged to his mother made into a bracelet to give as a bridal gift to Hannah.

And now, here he sat, no bracelet, no wife, waiting. Waiting for David to return from Hannah's home. Waiting to be well enough to make the trip back to that face.

David took his time walking out towards the sheepfold. This family had been so good to him, inviting him to stay longer, but he knew it was time to go. In the two days he had been here, he had grown particularly fond of the little one they called Nathaniel. He wanted to be sure to see him once more before he left, and he knew just where to find him. Every evening, as soon as the sheep had been brought in by Micah, Nathaniel was there waiting to play with the newest little lamb who had just recently been added back to the flock.

And there he was, just as David knew he would be.

As he drew nearer, David opened his mouth to call to the boy and then stopped suddenly, his attention caught by the boy's odd behavior. What was he doing?

David watched as the boy walked around what looked like a pile of rocks. The little lamb that most always accompanied the child these days, was following close behind as Nathaniel waved his hands and gave out orders to someone (though David could see no one) to pour water over the rocks. It was then that David noticed that a small ditch had been dug around the pile.

David was just about to step forward and disclose his presence when Nathaniel stopped walking abruptly. Curiosity drove David to conceal his presence a bit longer. He folded his arms and leaned against a tree. An amused smile tugged at his mouth as he watched the child take a deep breath, throw his head back, close his eyes, and fling his hands up into the air.

"Hear me O Lord!" Nathaniel's voice was as deep and solemn as one could imagine from a child so young.

Perplexed, David gave in to his curiosity and moved toward him as he called out, "What's that you're doing?"

Startled, Nathaniel jumped, and his eyes flew open. Still focused heavenward, he answered in a timid squeaky voice, "Waiting for your fire, Lord."

The burst of laughter that erupted drew the child's attention from the sky to David, now doubled over on the ground.

Glancing up with tears in his eyes from the strength of the laughter, David noticed the scowl on the boy's face as it registered that it was himself who seemed to the be the source of the big joke. David cleared his throat and bit his lip to hold back the laughter. "I'm sorry boy, but that is the first time I have ever been mistaken for God Almighty." His mouth was as straight and serious as he could muster, but his eyes still twinkled at the amusing thought.

After a moment, Nathaniel's face softened slightly as he realized the humor of the situation, and he allowed a small grin.

"Well, if you've forgiven me, may I be so bold as to ask why you were expecting fire?" David inquired as he strode closer to the boy.

Nathaniel drew his head back and blinked his eyes, shocked at the question. "I was being Elijah!"

David's forehead wrinkled, more perplexed than ever now. In the week since the big event had taken place, David had somehow managed to escape any knowledge of the outcome of Elijah's call to the mountain. Having no interest in what had taken place at the gathering atop Mount Carmel, he had never asked, and assuming there was no one who was unaware of the events, no one had ever offered the information; so this answer of Nathaniel's which seemed so simple to the child, made no connection in the mind of the thoroughly confused David. The look on his face must have effectively conveyed this confusion, because, after a moment, Nathaniel sighed with exasperation and began a more thorough explanation.

"I was doing just like Elijah did on Mount Carmel when he prayed, and God sent fire down to burn up the sacrifice and the water." The boy folded his arms over his chest, certain now that David must understand.

But instead of the knowing look that Nathaniel expected from David, a very different expression met the child's gaze. David's mouth had dropped open and his eyes had widened.

"God did what?" David asked, falling to his knees in front of the child to meet his steady gaze.

"Didn't you go and see?"

"No. No, I didn't." David shook his head from side to side.

Nathaniel's eyes lit up at the chance to relay the events of that day he was certain he would never forget. He took a deep breath and began to tell the story.

For the whole of the narration, David just knelt and listened, nodding every now and then, but never interrupting, and never taking his eyes off the animated child, until the entire story had been told.

". . . and then all the prophets of Baal got killed, but my dad wouldn't let me stay to see that part. And that's all."

David sat back on his heels and closed his eyes.

Fire from heaven.

"So, you say the fire fell as soon as Elijah prayed?"

Nathaniel cocked his head to one side, pausing to remember, and then nodded.

David's mind was reeling. God was paying attention.

"Hannah! Guess what! David didn't know about the fire coming down, but I told him."

"Oh really?" Hannah, who had just arrived to get Nathaniel for dinner, raised her eyebrows in surprise. "I thought that everyone had either seen or heard about it."

David just shook his head silently. Then he jumped up and turned toward Nathaniel. "Well, the very reason I came out to see you was to say goodbye. I really must be headed back to my mother, and, of course, Samuel." He turned his face toward Hannah and dropped his gaze. "I am glad to have been able to bring such good news to you."

"But it is so late! At least eat dinner with us."

No ma'am," David said quickly, "I must be getting home. Thank you for your hospitality." Then, ever so quickly, David turned and walked off.

Hannah stared after the retreating form.

"Why did he have to leave so soon?" Nathaniel asked.

Hannah turned to the sad boy and sat down on the ground beside him. She began stroking the lamb who had been contentedly sleeping throughout the entire exchange. "He just wanted to get back to his family, I suppose, as he said."

But she was not so certain herself. It was obvious that he had been troubled by something from the moment he had arrived, but he had seemed more so than ever this evening.

The lamb stirred beneath Hannah's fingers. So white. So pure.

"He's perfect, isn't he Hannah?"

Hannah nodded. Perfect. Just what God called for. The very best.

Hannah glanced over at the boy whose eyes held such absolute adoration for the animal. It was becoming more and more clear what the purpose of this lamb would be. And the boy had no idea.

~

"I want to be just like Elijah when I grow up!"

Joseph glanced down at the boy bounding along beside him as they made their way out to the threshing floor where the few stalks of barley had been laid out. It had been a small harvest, but he was thankful for what they had been able to reap. Today wooden threshing sledges would separate the grain from the chaff.

"Oh, and why is that?"

"He isn't afraid of anything! He was never afraid of King Ahab even though King Ahab always wanted to kill him. And there were a million prophets of Baal and just one of him at Mount Carmel and he wasn't afraid at all!"

"There weren't quite a million, Nathaniel, and I heard that as soon as Queen Jezebel heard what had happened, she was furious and threatened to kill him, and Elijah ran away. No one has seen him around since. It seems like he was feeling at least a little afraid then, and maybe still is."

Nathaniel stopped skipping and stood still for a moment, puzzled. "But I saw him when those mean prophets of Baal were dancing around! He wasn't afraid at all! He was just making fun of them, mocking them the whole time! How could he be afraid of just one mean lady?"

Joseph turned and knelt to look Nathaniel in the face. "I've been thinking about that very thing, Son. And I have been wondering about something. Why was he mocking those prophets?"

"What do you mean, Daddy?"

"When we choose to put someone else down or make fun of them, aren't we trying to make ourselves look better than them?"

"Well Elijah *is* better than them!"

"Is he? Was Elijah the one that kept himself safe from King Ahab all those years? Was it his power that kept it from raining? Or that kept him fed in the famine?"

"Well, no. It was God's power. But God always does what Elijah asks him to do."

"And why do you think that is?"

Nathaniel shrugged, "Because he's a prophet?"

"Because God chose it to be that way. Because God chose Elijah. Not the other way around. I am wondering if Elijah might have been forgetting that when he began mocking those prophets . . . if he might have been looking at his own strength rather than God's . . . if maybe in doing that, he began to rely on his own strength, and then when Jezebel made her threats, backed up by the strength of her armies, he was suddenly aware of his own weakness in comparison."

Nathaniel tilted his head to one side. "I don't get it, Daddy."

"Do you remember the day that you went out with Micah to help him with the sheep, and that lion came dangerously close to the flock?"

Nathaniel shivered at the memory. "Yes, I remember that day."

"What did you do?"

"I hid under Micah's camel hair coat."

"Exactly. And what did Micah do?"

"He took out his slingshot and killed the lion."

"So, what would have happened if you had decided to run out from his coat and mock the lion. What if you had run over to it and yelled, 'You silly lion! You're just a big dummy!'"

"Daddy! If I wasn't by Micah, the lion might have gotten me!"

"Exactly."

"So maybe Elijah ran out of God's coat?"

Joseph paused for a moment, looking up towards the clouds. "I don't know. But maybe."

7

> "Knowing that you were not redeemed with corruptible things, like silver and gold . . . but with the precious blood of Christ, as of a lamb without blemish and without spot:"

> I PETER 1:18A, 19 (NKJV)

A QUICK HIT TO the back of the head . . . blood streaming from the wound as he falls . . . dragging him to the ditch on the side of the road . . . grabbing the sack . . . running . . .

"Augh!"

David sat straight up, sweat pouring from his face. He looked around. No ditch. No blood. Only the quiet darkness and the twinkling stars above his head.

He lay back down. "Oh God! What have I done?" he whispered with a sob. His whole body trembled as he lay there, staring up at the sky.

He had told the family he was leaving to go home yesterday, but after Nathaniel's account of what had taken place on Mount Carmel, he was shaken. Badly shaken. He could not go back just yet. But neither could he stand to stay, and so he had decided to camp out just outside the village until he had sorted things out in his mind.

And he supposed this was the sorting.

"So, I guess you decided to remind me you know perfectly well what happened," David said to the silent stars with a short, bitter laugh as he thought back to that horrific night:

"We are not yet out of grain. God will provide," his mother had said.

"God will provide? Mother, you have said that almost every day since Father was taken. But where is the provision? Where is your God?" David had yelled as he had held up the almost empty bag of grain. "When are you going to realize that God does not care about us! He took your husband and now we are starving! If we are going to eat, I have to find some way to provide. Me. Not God. Me."

Then, throwing the bag down at her feet, David had stormed out of the hut.

The wind had been strong that evening and the dry earth threw up its dust at him as he had walked, head down, plodding forward. What could he do? He had spent the past year desperately trying to keep his father's fields producing, but to no avail. The small herd of sheep his father had managed to keep alive in the famine had been slaughtered months ago to keep himself and his mother alive. He had tried to hire himself out, but no one could afford to hire him.

Then he had seen him. A man was walking towards him on the road, head down to avoid the dust in his eyes. There was a leather bag around his waist.

A bag meant money most likely.

David had ducked behind a tree before the man had noticed him. As the man passed, David's mind had raced. Picking up a rock at his feet, he had stepped out onto the road behind the stranger and began to follow him.

Then he had stopped, his dad's last words echoing in his mind. "Trust God, Son, He is good."

Trust God? Trust God who had left him fatherless and hungry? No. He could not trust God. He had to rely on himself to provide for himself and his mother. He had no choice. With resolve he had raised the rock and run after the stranger . . .

The memory faded and the silent stars came back into focus. It seemed so strange to think that these same stars had looked down on the horrible thing he had done. Good, bad, the stars saw it all.

Yet they remained constant. Unchanged in their countenance towards a continually changing race. People rushing here and there. Loving. Hating. Mourning. Laughing. Yet the stars remained the stars. Silent. Giving twinkles of light in the darkness.

David lay there pondering what to do until he noticed the black of night retreating as a ribbon of gray dawn appeared on the horizon. Silent, motionless, David lay as the ribbon grew slowly brighter and pinker and swelled in the middle. At long last a burst of glaring light popped up at the swelling point sending streaks of light across the sky and over the dusty land. Yet all remained silent and still as though all creation stood in awe.

"What have I done?" David whispered. "I have sinned against the very creator of all of this. Of me!"

Slowly David lifted his body and positioned himself on his knees and bowed his head. "God, I have sinned against you. I had no faith. I tried to take care of it myself and look at the mess I made. And now I hear that you sent fire down when Elijah called to you. You have not forgotten. It is I who have forgotten. O God, forgive me."

Then he sat still, silently waiting.

Waiting for what? A punishment? For some sort of retribution to be announced from above?

He had sinned. He knew it. What was he to do now to make it right?

David's shoulders slumped and his arms fell limply to his sides. Nothing. He knew that nothing he could do would make it right. It was up to God now to show mercy and forgive . . . or not.

The silence of the morning rang in his ears. Would God forgive him?

"Turn from your ways! Repent!"

The words from a time far away came tumbling into his thoughts. His father, along with many other prophets, had cried these words to Israel for years. They had not been well received by this newest monarchy, but they had continued to be spoken boldly until Jezebel had done her best to silence those who spoke them.

Why would God tell people to repent if he did not intend to forgive them when they did?

A peace filled David's heart as he pondered this thought.

Well, repent he had done. Now he would just have to believe that God had forgiven him.

David rose from the dust, brushed off his knees and started off home to ask forgiveness of another.

∼

Joseph smiled as he stood watching his son from a little distance on this beautiful daybreak. There sat the child on the ground, laughing and playing with the lamb, up before the sun, as usual, wanting to watch God "push up" the big fiery ball.

The smile slowly faded as Joseph remembered why it was that he had come this beautiful morning to search for his son. He sighed deeply. "Hannah is right. I've got to tell him, and the sooner the better."

He stepped forward toward the boy and lamb.

"Nathaniel."

The boy stopped wrestling with the lamb and looked up at the sound of his name.

"Oh, hi Daddy! I didn't know you were here."

Joseph stooped down beside the boy.

"What's wrong Daddy?" asked Nathaniel noting the wrinkled brow.

"Nathaniel, do you remember our discussion the other day about how we would all be in trouble if God sent fire every time that we did something wrong?"

Nathaniel nodded; his eyes fixed intently on his father's face.

"Well, the fact is, God would have every right to knock us down dead every time we did something wrong. Every time we disobeyed him."

Nathaniel's eyes widened.

"This is because he is holy. And we are not."

"What does that mean Daddy?"

"It means God is perfect. He has not, nor ever will, do anything that is not good. But we do. Anything that we do wrong is directly against him, against his very nature. We hurt him every time we sin. He can't even look at sin, because he is so perfect. And, in the same way, we can't look at him or we would die, because he is so holy."

Nathaniel swallowed hard. "Then why doesn't he kill everybody?" he whispered softly, his eyes still locked on his father's face.

"Well, he loves us enough that he figured out a way for us to cover up our sins, so he could still be with us. That's what I really wanted to talk to you about . . . the way God set up for us to have our sins covered."

"How's that?"

"Well," Joseph looked over at the beautiful little lamb lying peacefully beside his son. "Something has to die."

"What do you mean?" Nathaniel said, grabbing the lamb and jumping up when he noticed where his father's gaze had fallen. He pulled the lamb to himself protectively.

"Nathaniel, the punishment for doing something against God is death. God loves the people that he made so much that he doesn't want them to die every time they sin, so he said we could kill something else in our place."

"What did he say to kill?" Nathaniel's voice shook a bit and he clutched the lamb more tightly.

"The very best, most perfect animal from our flock." Joseph leaned forward and laid his hand on his son's trembling shoulder. "A lamb, Nathaniel."

Nathaniel's eyes dropped and a single tear splashed onto the white wool.

Joseph continued softly, "Every year I take the most spotless lamb we have down to Jerusalem to the temple to be sacrificed for our family. Usually the whole family goes with me, but last year your mother was too weak to travel and so you stayed here with her, and the year before you were too young to remember. But I laid a hand on the head of the lamb last year for both you and your mother. This year you will go, though I'm not sure your mother will be able to."

"Shalom is the most perfect one, isn't he?" Nathaniel's voice was almost too soft to hear.

Joseph paused for a moment feeling heavily the grief of his son.

"Yes, Nathaniel. This lamb is as spotless as they come."

Suddenly the boy fiercely shook his father's hand from his shoulder and cried, "But it's not his fault! He didn't do anything wrong!"

Joseph just sat quietly, gazing steadily into the pained eyes of the boy.

Nathaniel stood glaring back down at him for a moment longer before turning to run towards the house, the lamb still tightly in his grasp, shouting, "It's not fair! He didn't sin!"

Joseph shook his head slowly as he watched the distraught boy run away. "No," he whispered, "it is not fair. Thank God it is not fair."

~

Abbigail was crying for her dinner when Hannah handed her to her mother. "How are you feeling today, Mama?"

Miriam shifted her weight on the bed to position the baby to her breast. "Well, dear, I am feeling very full of joy for you and Samuel."

Hannah's face brightened at the mention of the name Samuel. It was good to have a happy jump of her stomach with the name again.

"Yes, it is such good news! And that dear boy who brought us the news! He says he and his widowed mother live alone, so I thought maybe we could ask them to stay with us for a while when Samuel returns. I think it might help to ease some of the responsibility he must feel for his mother."

"Of course, dear." Miriam smiled. "And I could certainly use the help with the baby. The servants have so much to do as it is, and with you preparing to leave soon . . ."

"I've been wanting to talk to you about that, Mama," Hannah interrupted.

Miriam looked up at her oldest daughter. She knew her daughter well enough to know that at some point guilt would strike this conscientious girl who had been so good to her, and she was prepared for this talk. She patted the side of the mat on which she lay. "Hannah, come sit with me."

Hannah knelt beside her mother. "Mama, I just think that it might be best for Samuel and I to wait before marrying. You have grown so much weaker in the past few weeks, and I just think . . ."

Miriam put a hand on Hannah's arm to stop her. "Listen child. I knew there was some trouble carrying this child even before the delivery. I knew it would probably greatly weaken me to have a child at all. I was never very strong even after Nathaniel. You know that. Last year, even before I knew of Abbigail's presence, I was sick much of the time. Remember?"

Hannah nodded her head and a tear clung to her eyelash.

"My body just fights the beautiful process of bearing children for some reason. I knew that before Samuel ever disappeared. It is good that you marry, child, and there is no man I would rather see you with than your Samuel. And you will be living quite close. You can get here easily if we need you too."

"But Mama!" Hannah buried her head in her mother's lap. "How will you get up for the ceremony? I cannot bear to think that you won't be there to see it!"

Miriam stroked the dark head. "God will work all of that out, child. Don't you worry yourself about me."

Hannah raised her head as the baby began to wiggle at the intruder on her mother's lap. She smiled as Abbigail went back to suckling contently. "Well, Abbigail does not seem to be worried!"

Miriam looked down at the suckling baby who lay content and trusting so completely the arms that held her tight. "May we all be like this child."

～

Samuel hardly noticed the rush of wind and darkening of the sky as he walked slowly trying to settle the jumble of thoughts and emotions that had not left his brain since David's confession earlier that morning.

He had been hit on the head with a rock and robbed by the very person he had believed to be his rescuer; this information was having a hard time finding a place of rest in his mind.

He looked down at the bracelet in his hand, the bracelet he had bought for his beloved Hannah. David had told him that he planned to repay him four times what the bracelet was worth in recompense for the theft, but Samuel's emotions refused to be pacified; he had been assaulted and then deceived. The injury from the physical assault was one thing, but the injury from the deception felt like an even deeper assault to his pride. He had believed the story that David had found him hurt in the ditch. He had thanked him numerous times for his care. And, worst of all, he had trusted him, a thief, to give the news to Hannah and her family.

Samuel's fist tightened around the bracelet as a wave of anger surged through his body, and his steps quickened until they broke into a run. A rumble of thunder in the distance seemed to echo the grumble of his spirit as he tried to outrun his anger.

It was not long before his recently injured body could not match the intensity of his emotions, and Samuel stumbled over to a tree to sit down and rest just as the clouds above him burst open. He pulled his knees up to his chest and looked up at the leaves above him which offered little shelter from the heavy shower.

Samuel shivered. Logic told him that he should just be thankful that things had not turned out as badly as they could have, thankful that his head injury had healed, thankful that he had the bracelet back.

But he was not feeling thankful. He was feeling angry, and resentful. And he wanted some form of retribution.

David's apology had seemed sincere, Samuel admitted to himself; he had seemed truly sorry for his deeds and ready to make whatever amends he could. But that was not enough. Samuel had been seriously injured. An apology did not satisfy.

He had left the small hut simply to cool off and think, but now, as he sat, soaked to the skin, Samuel determined that he would not go back. He was certain he was well enough to make the trip home. And the thought of looking at the face of the deceiver and thief made him feel sick.

With this new resolve, and the adrenalin that comes with intense emotion on his side, Samuel rose and set off with determination toward home.

~

Nathaniel sat, silently stroking the soft wool as he watched the clouds of the recent storm move off into the distance. There was no laughing or playing today. Just silence. Heavy silence.

The lamb stood up and rubbed his nose into the boy's cheek.

"Oh Shalom!" Nathaniel wrapped his small arms around the woolly neck. "Why do you have to be so perfect? Why do you have to die?"

The lamb just snuggled cozily into the boy's arms, undisturbed by the death sentence that hung over his fuzzy little head. Nathaniel clung more tightly. There they sat, the miserable boy and his lamb.

Nathaniel looked up at the clouds floating by.

"Why, God?" he whispered. "Why would you want this lamb killed? He's just so little, and he hasn't done anything wrong."

Nathaniel began to stroke the soft back that was rising and falling slowly with the even breaths of the animal who so exemplified his name. Shalom. Peace. It is well. Nathaniel sighed as the soft head laid itself down in his lap.

"Don't you understand? You are going to die! You are the best we've got, the perfectest of all the others, and so you are going to get killed!"

The lamb remained still, silent, seemingly unaffected by the raised voice and waving arms of the boy.

Once more the boy's eyes raised to the sky.

"Why God? Why would you ask for the best to die? What did Shalom ever do wrong that he would deserve to die?"

Nathaniel dropped his gaze to the spotless white of the wooly body.

Nothing. The lamb had done nothing wrong.

"But I have." It was barely a whisper, but the lamb raised his head to look up into the teary eyes of the boy who had uttered the words.

"It's because of me. You don't do wrong stuff, but I do. That's why you have to die. It's so I don't have to."

~

Samuel stood silently on the other side of the fence watching the weeping boy, having arrived in time to hear most of the dialogue. He had witnessed the sacrificial lamb numerous times in his life, but the boy's interactions had stirred something deep within his soul.

Samuel had always thought of himself as a decent man; he lived an honest life and always did his best to help others. But listening to the boy seemed to uncover the deep truth and reveal the hidden things of his heart.

He hung his head as buried sins rose to the surface of his mind: anger that God had let his mother and father die, resentment that Micah still had a family while he was all alone, selfishness that wanted Hannah all to himself even though he knew her mother needed her . . . *pride that thought he was better than the man who had stolen from him.*

As Samuel stood there silently, he realized, for the first time in his life, that he deserved to die; that set up against the perfect standard of a holy God, Samuel did not stand a chance.

A conversation Samuel had had with his father shortly before he had died came to his mind:

"There is no way a lamb can actually take the punishment for a human!" Samuel had said skeptically.

"I agree," his father had said. "I am certain it simply represents a bigger truth, a truth we cannot fully comprehend. We sacrifice the lamb out of obedience. By that act of obedience, we are admitting that we are sinful, that we deserve to die, that we need a substitute for our deserved punishment, and that, somehow, God will take care of the bigger truth that we cannot understand; He will, someday, cover it with more than just a lamb."

Samuel's thoughts then turned back to David. A wave of bitterness had to be shoved aside to consider the truth of the situation:

Samuel had reason to be angry with David.

God had reason to be angry with Samuel.

Samuel had been wronged by David.

God had been wronged by Samuel.

God had plenty of reasons to be angry, and yet he chose to forgive; God had been wronged over and over, and yet he chose to make a way for Samuel to be saved from the deserved punishment. How could Samuel continue to accept the love and forgiveness of a perfect holy God, and yet determine not to give the same back to David?

Samuel shook his head as the truth of it sunk in, and he said aloud, "I forgive him."

Two things happened simultaneously with the utterance of those words. First, Samuel felt a heavy weight lift from his heart. Second, the weeping boy, who heard the words and suddenly realized that his beloved friend had come back, dropped the lamb and raced over to greet him.

"Samuel!" Nathaniel's face lit up as he jumped into the arms of Samuel and threw his arms around his neck. Then his face drew back, and he said with a very serious expression, "Who do you forgive?"

Samuel just laughed and held the precious boy close. He knew that after a night's rest, or maybe two, he needed to head back and tell David that he had forgiven him.

8

"Let us be glad and rejoice and give Him glory, for the marriage of the Lamb has come, and His wife has made herself ready."

REVELATION 19:7 (NKJV)

HANNAH STROKED THE SOFT linen of the robe that draped around her as she admired the fine gold embroidered so delicately into it. She twirled around feeling the soft folds as they caressed her legs beneath the beautiful fabric. She wrapped the gold and silver bracelets around her arm, pausing to smile at the one Samuel had brought to her, and then fastened the gold nose ring in its place.

Adorning herself for her groom. Again.

"You are a beautiful bride, my child."

Hannah turned, startled. "Mama! You are out of bed!"

"You do not think I'd miss this do you?" Her eyes sparkled, but Hannah could see that a tiredness behind them betrayed the weakness of the body.

"Mama, sit down." Hannah rushed over to help her mother onto a mat on the floor in the small room.

Miriam allowed herself to be gently pushed down onto the mat. "I saw some of the girls out there already, lamps in hand."

Hannah sighed, remembering the last time they had come and waited with her. She sat down on the mat beside her mother, drew her knees up, and placed her chin in her hands.

"Don't worry about them, dear," Miriam patted her daughter's hand. "You knew then that he would come, as you know now."

Hannah stood to her feet and threw up her hands. "But Mama! He didn't come, and they all know it!"

Miriam sat silently for a moment; her eyes fixed steadily on her distraught daughter. Then she spoke quietly, but firmly. "Not in your timing, no, and you now know exactly why."

Hannah let her hands drop and she took her seat once again beside her mother, eyes staring straight ahead. No, certainly, in her timing he had not come.

"But he is coming," Miriam continued, taking Hannah's chin in her hand and turning it to face her own. She smiled before adding, "And even then, he was coming."

Hannah turned away, finding no humor in the situation.

"You are well aware of the reason for his delay. As surely now, as then, he is coming to get you and make you his bride. What those other girls think about it does not change that fact. It is just your pride that is hurt."

Hannah turned back to her frail, but ever so serene mother and smiled sheepishly. "I know. Thank you for reminding me." Then her eyes clouded. "You are not able to get to the feast though, are you."

Miriam's eyes danced. "Well, actually your father has hooked up an ox to an old cart, and he is planning to lead me over in that. It's only just down the road you know."

"Oh Mama! I am so glad!" Hannah cried, throwing her arms around her tightly.

"Of course, I will not be able to stay for the full week of festivities, but," she added quickly, "that sweet mother of David's is going to stay here with me, so I will be fine. Don't you worry about me."

"She is a kind woman, isn't she Mama?"

"A wonderfully kind woman. And been through a lot to have kept such a pleasant disposition."

"How do you think she did it, Mama? Remain so cheerful after losing first her husband so violently, and then just about everything else in the drought?"

"It is the peace of God, child. It is beyond understanding, but it is real. And quite evident in that woman's life," Miriam said closing her eyes and nodding her head as though she understood that peace very well herself.

"Well, I certainly like her," Hannah affirmed.

"And I am glad her son could be a part of the festivities. It was good of Samuel to ask him," Miriam added opening her eyes and glancing over at her daughter.

Hannah rose from the mat slowly and turned away, fiddling with her hair. "Mmm, yes. Good of him."

Miriam watched quietly for a moment as her daughter mindlessly twisted the long braid. "You have not forgiven him."

Hannah continued to fiddle with the braid. "Of course, I have. I told him so when he asked it of me a week ago."

"But you continue to remind him of his sin every time you see him."

Hannah turned towards her mother and put her hands on her hips. "Mama! What are you talking about? I have not said anything at all to him about it!"

Miriam gazed steadily into the flushed face. "My child, every flash of your eyes, every dismissal of his conversation, every convenient excuse to be anywhere but where he is lets him know that you have not forgotten, and therefore, he may not either."

Hannah turned again, unable to meet her mother's gaze. "I just cannot help but picture him hitting my Samuel every time I look at him."

Miriam lifted a hand to take hold of her daughter's arm. "I know, my child. I know."

"There you are!"

Hannah and Miriam turned to see the energetic Rachel in the doorway.

"I was wondering where you would be getting ready. Almost everyone is here and ready now. They are all excited! I was talking to Sarah just moments ago and you would never know it was she who left first the last time the way she was going on and on about how she always knew he would come for you. I just smiled and then made my exit as quickly as possible, afraid I might say something I would regret later." Rachel's hands were waving around dramatically as she continued, "All the girls are saying that now, you know. 'We knew he would come! We knew he had a good reason for not coming the last time!'"

Suddenly Rachel's eyes grew wide and she ran to her friend, reaching out to touch the detail of the gold embroidered pattern on her gown. "Oooo! I had almost forgotten what a beautiful gown it was!"

Hannah laughed at her friend's enthusiasm.

Her friend.

Yes, Rachel was truly her friend. It was Rachel who had remained with her that whole night and most of the next day the last time. It had been Hannah, herself, who had finally convinced her that she must go home. And for the next few weeks, while whispers of what had kept Samuel flew through the village, Rachel had held her tongue, though a great task that had been, and replied only, "He will come," to the various rumors, repeating in faith the phrase that had been continually on Hannah's own lips.

Now here she was back and ready for another night of it.

Yes, God had given her a good friend in this energetic girl who was now at her feet feeling the soft badger's skin of her wedding slippers.

∼

The moon cast its beam through the one window of the small room, splashing softly across the veil spread over the cedar table located in the center of the room.

Hannah sat watching the steady breathing of her mother's sleep. She twisted the bracelets around her arm, listening to the gold clanking against the silver.

"Sleep Mama," she had urged her as the night had grown dark and silent. She knew that though she pretended renewed energy this evening of her daughter's marriage, she was exhausted.

It had grown quite late, and Hannah had noticed long before that the laughter and chatting of the girls waiting outside had ceased. They, too, were sleeping, no doubt.

But no sleep would come this night to her own tense body.

He was taking a long time. Again.

Hannah shook her head to throw off such thoughts of the last time. He would come, just as her mother had said. She looked down again at her mother sleeping peacefully. Hannah smiled at the determination of this woman, her own dear mother. She knew that much of the time she was in pain, but Hannah had yet to hear a complaint. She knew that it was hard to watch others take much of the responsibility for her own infant, but only smiles of gratitude greeted those who helped with Abbigail. She knew she may not be here on the earth much longer, but never a despairing word slipped from her lips.

Hannah felt a tear drop from her cheek onto her mother's thin arm. It was not going to be easy to live without her.

Hannah's head flew up as she heard a sound in the night. It was coming from outside the house. She flew to her feet and grabbled the veil from the table, quickly attaching it to her head with the combs. She could hear the beating of her own heart in her ears as she held her breath and waited.

A moment later Rachel's head popped through the doorway. By the light of the lamp she held in her hands, Hannah could see that her eyes were dancing. "He's here. Hannah, he's come for you."

Never had more precious words reached Hannah's ears. Her heart leapt and she drew the veil over her face, taking a step forward. Then, remembering her mother, she leaned down lifting her veil to kiss her cheek before leaving.

Stirred awake by the commotion, Miriam's eyes opened. "I love you my child. Shalom. Go in peace."

And go she did. Stomach fluttering, and knees shaking, Hannah stepped out into the night where the dancing lights of oil lamps and cheering friends greeted her.

There were so many people, all shouting and dancing as the procession approached, and Hannah grew suddenly overwhelmed with the realization that they were all here for her. This was her night. She felt her heart beat faster and her hands grow damp as she folded and unfolded them, waiting for what came next.

Then she saw him.

He stood leading the parade of young men and women. On his head was a splendid diadem. His very best robe was wrapped tightly around him, and his face was lit with love and adoration for the one he had chosen. Then he stepped forward to meet his bride.

The noise and lights of the crowd faded into the night as Hannah gazed through her veil into the eyes of her beloved. Her heartbeat slowed, and her knees stopped shaking.

This was peace. Her beloved had come at last.

∼

Day one of the festivities had begun. The ceremony had taken place the night before as soon as Samuel had escorted his bride from her house to his own, followed by a throng of dancing, singing friends. The wedding songs had been sung, and then the friends had left in the night while Samuel took his bride into the privacy of his home and made her his wife.

Now the feasting had begun. Sheep had been slaughtered and roasted for the occasion, and every sort of fruit and nut garnished the tables. There would be seven days of music and games and dancing before the wedding would be over. Harps, lyres, and tambourines could be heard throughout the village as all came to celebrate this joining together of man and wife.

"Look at how happy they look. Did you see Hannah's face when she saw Samuel?"

Athalia took the flute down from her lips and looked up at Rachel whose eyes had never left the bride and groom since the beginning of the feast. "How could you see her face? She had a veil on."

Rachel smiled and sighed shaking the tambourine in her hand. "But you could just tell, you know? There was a sort of glow. Too bad I will never know that feeling."

Athalia began to play the flute again. The sweet sound of it flowed beautifully with the other instruments until a tug at her arm interrupted her once more.

"There he is, the one whom I am being forced to marry. Isn't he just so . . . so lifeless?"

Exasperated Athalia lowered her flute once again to follow the direction of Rachel's pointing finger. Maybe if she just looked and nodded, Rachel would go back to dancing and let her play the flute. She glanced over into the crowd and began to nod, pretending to see the infamous Elihu.

Suddenly, she froze. Athalia's mouth flew open and the flute slipped from her fingers. The strangely familiar nauseous feeling rose in her chest. People were singing and dancing all around her now, but she could not move. Everything seemed to be moving in slow motion. The sounds of the instruments and voices grew dim as the beating of her own heart pulsed faster and louder in her ears. Could it really be?

At that moment, the man who had captured her attention turned, and his cold eyes met her own. The sickeningly familiar sneer met her gaze, and she knew she had been caught.

Without thinking, Athalia turned and, picking up the hem of her tunic, ran.

"So what do you think? Isn't there something so . . ." Rachel, who had been dancing again and had not noticed Athalia's quick exit looked around and around, trying to locate her friend in the crowd. "Athalia? Where did that girl go?"

❧

Athalia fell to the ground, exhausted. Her heart was beating wildly, and her breath came in deep gulps. She rubbed her sore feet which the sticks and rocks of the forest floor had thoroughly bruised in the run.

"Oh, little one! What are we going to do now? I'm certain he recognized me. We will be found out for sure!" She laid a hand on the slightly swelling belly. "And if he doesn't tell, shouldn't I? I mean it wouldn't be fair to Rachel to not warn her. What am I going to do?"

Athalia lay her head back against the trunk of a sycamore tree and closed her eyes. As the sound of her own breathing slowed, she could faintly hear the happy music from the wedding festivities in the distance. Happy music. All were caught up in the couple's joy.

It was as it should be for Hannah and Samuel. The party continued without her, and no one had noticed her exit . . .

"So! The harlot has left the temple!"

Athalia's eyes flew open and her hand rose protectively to her belly as the sickening voice pierced the air.

The action did not go unnoticed by the huge man standing over her. His bulbous form, belly hanging in loose folds over the belt that held his tunic at the waist, could be mistaken for no other. The Hebrew from the temple. Elihu. They were one and the same. His face twisted into a sneer as he leaned over the terrified girl, grabbing her wrist and flinging it from her belly. He lowered his own fleshy hand to caress the soft body of the shaking girl, feeling the slight rise of what he knew used to be a flat stomach. Athalia's skin crawled at the familiar touch.

"Ah. So, you're with child, I see. Ran away thinking you could save your bastard baby? Is that it? The temple prostitute risking her life to save her baby! How touching!"

Athalia stared in wide eyed terror at the hideous face above her. "Please don't hurt my baby," she whispered.

Then he smiled, an evil twisted thing, and leaned toward her until his face was just inches away from the pale, terrified one and whispered, "Then you'd better think twice before telling anyone what you know about me. If you so much as hint to anyone that I have, on occasion, made a visit to your temple, I cannot guarantee the safety of you or your bastard baby. Do you understand?"

Athalia nodded her head vigorously as a tear escaped one wide, frightened eye.

Elihu leaned towards her, enjoying her discomfort immensely. Then he leaned back.

"What did you think? That you could just become a part of this family and maybe they would save your baby? You are a harlot! That is what you are. A wicked, disgusting sinner. There is no changing that."

With that, he picked up his massive form and began to walk away from the shaking girl. Then he turned, and with a wicked gleam in his eye he said, "And what do you think your new friends would think of your bastard baby if they knew the truth?"

Athalia turned her head as a tear dropped to the ground.

Elihu turned again and walked away, unaware of the form crouched low in the brush as he walked past.

∽

"Bastard baby? The truth?" David's mind whirled around the strange question he had overheard.

Athalia's exit had not been nearly as discreet as she had hoped. David, being fully enamored by the music from the little wooden flute, and rather attracted, as well, to the girl playing it, had positioned himself near enough to hear the beautiful sound but far enough away to not attract attention. He had been deeply engrossed in the sweet melody with his eyes closed when the sound had abruptly stopped. He had opened his eyes in time to see the flute drop and the odd look of horror on the musician's face right before she had run off. Curious, he had pushed his way through the crowd of dancers and musicians to retrieve the flute, nearly getting trampled in the process, and started off in the direction she had disappeared.

What he had not noticed was that the large, gruff man who had been standing beside him was just as interested and had taken off after the girl while David retrieved the flute.

She had disappeared down the village street and into fields behind the village. David had wandered, rather aimlessly, hoping to run into the obviously frightened girl to see if he might be able to help. Just as he was ready to give up the search, he had heard a voice coming from a small clump of sycamore trees. It was low and gruff and certainly not the voice of the small girl whom he pursued, but curiosity made him turn and follow it. When he had heard the final words, he realized that he had stumbled upon some sort of a rendezvous and ducked into some heavy brush, just in time it turned out, for the large man whose voice he had heard turned toward him and walked out of the clearing just as he ducked.

David's eyebrows drew together as he tried to place the familiar face of the man who had walked past him. Where had he seen him?

Then he saw her.

Her legs were drawn up to her chest with her arms pulled tightly around them, and her face was buried down into them. Her whole body shook with sobs.

What was this all about? Who was that man who seemed to know more about this girl than anyone else? And what about this baby he was talking about? David did not remember seeing a child with this girl, although, he realized, he only knew very little about her himself. After she had taken him to Hannah's house on the day he had delivered the news of Samuel, he had not seen much of her at all.

Obviously whatever had transpired was causing the girl a good deal of distress, and David, not wishing to cause more by letting her know he had seen or heard anything, quietly left the clearing, and made his way back to the wedding feast.

~

"Now what little one?" It was growing dark as Athalia sat resting against the tree. She had not moved since the horrifying encounter with Elihu. The threat of harm to herself and her child played over and over in her mind. Why had he not just killed her right there so as not to take any chances of her telling his own secret?

Athalia shook her head. Whatever the reason, he had left her unharmed, physically anyway, to decide the next step on her own.

What were her options?

Her first impulse was to run far away; who was to say that Elihu would not get fearful of exposure and kill her to ensure the secrecy? She needed to get as far away from him as possible.

But where?

Returning to the temple was not an option, or anywhere in Samaria for that matter. She was sure to be recognized there. And on her own out here, she would surely die.

Athalia leaned her head back with a deep sigh realizing that she was merely choosing her own demise, either at the hand of Elihu or nature.

Then she leaned forward as she felt a flutter in her belly. Her hand rose to feel it. There it was again. Her eyes widened and a surprised laugh erupted from her mouth. She could feel her child! He was moving inside of her, and she could feel his little life!

Suddenly her decision seemed of the utmost importance. She needed to decide based on what option would make it most likely that this baby's little life would continue.

This really left only one option open. She must return to Hannah's home as if nothing had happened. Possibly Elihu would remain true to his word and leave her alone if she kept her mouth shut. And that is just what she would have to do. She would join the festivities again and hope that in the commotion of the wedding feast, no one would have noticed her absence to ask any questions.

And of Elihu, she would forget she even knew him.

But what about Rachel?

Athalia's head fell back again against the tree and her eyes closed. If she said nothing, the betrothal would commence, and poor Rachel would be stuck for life serving that wretched man.

But who was Rachel to her? Was she more important than this child in her?

Athalia's head spun.

And who was to say that if she did tell all she knew of Elihu that Rachel would not be forced to marry him still? Besides, if he married her, he would have no reason to keep going to the temple of Baal. Maybe he would end up being a good husband to her.

No, she must save her child. She could not tell.

With the decision made, Athalia picked herself up and headed back to the festivities.

9

*After this I looked, and behold, a great multitude which no one
could number, of all nations, tribes, peoples, and tongues, standing
before the throne and before the Lamb, clothed with white robes,
with palm branches in their hands,"*

REVELATION 7:9 (NKJV)

"AND I GOT TO walk with them in the parade all the way to Samuel's
house in the middle of the night! They even gave me a tambourine to shake! I think almost everyone from the village was there.
Everyone held a lamp so we could see down the street. Even Mama
came in a cart. Daddy walked by her."

Nathaniel was especially animated this afternoon and the
lamb tried, to no avail, to get comfortable in the excited boy's arms
which were anything but still.

"There was so much singing and dancing! And Hannah
looked so beautiful in her pretty dress. I think Samuel was the
happiest though. He didn't ever stop smiling the whole way to his
house. I couldn't see Hannah's face 'cause she had to wear a veil.
But we all made a lot of noise going down the street. It's a good
thing most of the village was there, or they would have been mad,
I bet, if they were trying to sleep or something. When we got there,
we sang a lot of songs for them, and then we left. But then for
the whole next week we got to have a party at their new house!
There was so much food and dancing and singing every single day.

Mama even let me stay up late most of those nights, but Jerusha always had to take me home to sleep.

"She stays with us now, you know. Samuel asked them to come to the wedding, and Mama liked Jerusha so much that Daddy asked them if they could stay, so Jerusha could help Mama, and David could help Daddy and Micah in the fields and with the sheep. They don't really have anything left back where they live, so they said okay.

"I don't see David much cause he's always with Daddy, but Jerusha is really nice. She smiles all the time and laughs a lot. Like Mama. I think that's why Mama likes her so much. She mostly takes care of baby Abbigail now that Hannah is gone."

Then Nathaniel's smile faded, and his body grew still. The lamb took advantage of the quiet moment, settling comfortably into the suddenly calm lap.

"Mama is getting worse. I think that's really why Daddy asked Jerusha to stay, so someone could take care of Abbigail when Mama . . ." A sob caught in his throat. Then his little head drew back fiercely.

"If only she hadn't been born!" he said through clenched teeth.

～

"Hannah, David came by earlier this morning. He says he has something important to discuss with you."

"Hmm, something important?" Hannah did not look up from the weaving loom.

Samuel sighed and sat down next to his new bride. "Hannah, this has got to stop."

Hannah set the spindle of wool down and looked up at her husband. "What has to stop?"

Samuel reached over and took her hand. "I know that it was hard for you, not knowing why I did not come for you, and then finding out why, but it is over now. I am fine. You are my wife. You must let go of it."

Hannah's eyes dropped, and her free hand began to draw designs in the dust of the floor.

Samuel took his hand and gently raised her chin to look again into his own face. "David feels terribly about what he has done, and he has asked forgiveness of God. Do you think that God has refused?"

Hannah's eyes filled with tears and she jumped to her feet. "I just don't know how! When I see him, I see you being hurt! You could have been killed! I try to be nice to him, but I just can't!" she cried, and then, with a sob turned and ran. She ran and ran, away from the hut that had just recently become her home, away from her husband who was disappointed with her unforgiveness.

She had run for quite some time before she realized that her body, overcome with emotion, had brought her straight to the little sheepfold by her father's field. Her tired body collapsed right by the door of the stone enclosure. Her tired heart was out of tears, so she just leaned back against the door, dry-eyed and expressionless.

After some time, she felt a gentle nudge against her hip. Glancing down she saw the soft eyes of the lamb looking up at her. A slight dip in the soil made just enough room under the door for him to push his head under.

Shalom. Fitting name for the animal that would make a way for there to be peace between God and her family, Hannah thought to herself. She rubbed the little head.

"He has asked forgiveness of God. Do you think that God has refused?"

The words of Samuel played over and over in her mind as she stroked the soft wool.

Of course, Hannah knew, God had not refused. That was the whole point of the Passover lamb, the redeemer. We do bad things, and God provided a way for us to be at peace with him anyway.

Hannah gathered her knees up to her chest and buried her face in her hands. "I just want him to hurt, like he hurt me and Samuel," Hannah whispered to the lamb.

All was silent for a moment.

Then an odd thought passed over her mind. She raised her head to the clear blue sky. "Does my sin hurt God?"

Hannah dropped her head and looked at the little lamb, still craning its neck, wiggling as far as it could manage to get itself under the wooden board. "Do you think that God actually hurts when we do wrong things? Do you think that my actions cause him grief? Does he hurt like I am hurting?"

Why would the God of the universe put in place a system to make peace with the very creation that he knew would just hurt him over and over and over? And how many times had she, herself, hurt him by her own actions?

"Hannah."

Hannah jumped to her feet and spun around.

"I'm sorry, I did not mean to startle you."

There stood David, head down, gaze to the ground.

Hannah braced herself and forced a smile, trying hard to remember her husband's gentle reprimand.

"It's about your friend Athalia . . ."

Hannah's head cocked to one side and she nodded for him to continue.

"Well, I don't know if I should be saying anything, but I thought that since you have been such a good friend to her that maybe you could find out if here is any way to help her. Of course, I am not quite sure she needs help, but I think something is wrong."

David paused for a moment, pacing in front of Hannah before flinging his hands up in the air. "I'm sorry, I will just tell you what I heard, and you can do with it what you like. I noticed that she ran off from your wedding feast last week, so I followed her, and I found her leaning against a tree sobbing. Some man was just leaving her saying something about people knowing the truth about her and her baby . . ."

Hannah's eyes widened. "Go on."

David shrugged, "That's all I know. I left without her ever seeing me. She has no idea I know even that much. But you should have seen her face. She was terrified!"

Hannah's brow wrinkled.

"Can you help her somehow?" David's eyes pleaded.

"I think it would be best to let her tell her secret in her own time. If we were to push her, she might run away again."

"Again?" David looked at her questioningly.

"I'm just guessing, because of the way I found her, that she has run away from somewhere. I say we just treat her as always and let her decide when she feels secure enough to tell us. Nothing could possibly be too big for God to take care of and forgive if necessary . . ." her voice trailed off as her brain registered her own words. She glanced up into the troubled face in front of her.

David's gaze dropped.

"Thank you for telling me," Hannah said finally, breaking the uncomfortable silence.

David nodded and turned to go.

As he walked away, Hannah looked up and whispered, "Oh God, help me to forgive him."

~

Athalia had just finished cleaning up after the noon meal when Rachel found her. She had been by to see her almost every day since the wedding festivities had ended a week ago. As Hannah's wife status had kept her a bit more occupied, Rachel had found someone new upon whom to relieve her dire need to express herself.

Athalia saw her coming from a distance and sighed. It was time to put on the polite smile and listen to the day's news. She fought every day, determined to keep from really liking this girl, so full of life and joy, who had been so nice to her lately. Should she grow fond of her, it would be far harder to keep the secret. She set the cleaning rag into a bowl of water as Rachel approached.

"Athalia, it has finally come. I have dreamed my whole life about this, and now it's here, though not quite as I'd hoped it would be."

Athalia braced herself for the hug that always accompanied the girl's opening statement.

Today, however, the hug never came. Rachel merely plopped herself down on the ground and waited for Athalia to join her.

Taken aback by the less than joyful greeting, Athalia lowered herself slowly to the ground beside her. "Is everything alright?"

Rachel chewed on her bottom lip and doodled in the dirt at her feet. "Mmmm. All right? Yes, I suppose everything is all right. It's just . . . hard."

Athalia sat silently waiting for her to continue.

"The betrothal is set for the day after tomorrow. Elihu has the bridal gifts prepared. My father's wife is most excited about that part . . . the gifts I mean." Rachel rolled her eyes as the words left her mouth.

"Anyway, it's all set. I will be a betrothed woman in two days. Committed. Of course, I do have a year to get completely used to the idea. Elihu will go back to Shechem to wait out the betrothal period."

Athalia's eyes lit up at this news. Shechem was a good distance from Samaria. "Shechem?"

"Yes, that is where he is from, you know. He came at my stepmother's request. He's a distant cousin of hers or something. 'He's a good man, solid and upright,' she had told my father, who, of course, would never allow his daughter to marry anything less."

Rachel was too caught up in her own monologue to notice the expression that shot across Athalia's face at these last words.

"He's rich, you know. Says I won't have to do a bit of work as his wife. He has oodles of servants, I guess. I suppose my only real job will be to have babies. Oh, that reminds me!" Rachel turned suddenly toward Athalia, and there was a slight spark in her eyes for the first time since she had arrived. "Elihu says I can bring someone with me to be a nursemaid if I want, you know, someone to help out with all the kids he's planning to have. Anyway, I was wondering if you would come with me. I didn't know, but I was guessing you don't have any family around?"

Athalia's eyes fell to her belly.

"Oh, I'm sorry! I didn't mean to . . ."

"No." Athalia took a deep breath and raised her gaze again to Rachel. "You are correct. I do not."

"Well, I just thought that maybe . . . you'd have your own room and even your own servants . . ." Rachel looked questioningly into the carefully guarded eyes that looked so evenly back at her, revealing nothing.

She sighed and turned back to her doodling. "It was selfish of me, really, to ask. I just wanted to have at least one person I could talk to. And I do so love to talk with you. But, of course, someone as young and pretty as yourself would want to get married and have your own children. I would hate for both of us to be miserable."

Athalia stared, speechless. Rachel had obviously come from great wealth herself, and now she was asking Athalia, nothing more than a poor stranger, to come and take part in her soon to be richer life. And she was saying it was selfish of her?

Mistaking Athalia's expression for that of pity, Rachel quickly put on a smile and sat up straight. "But don't worry about me! I was quite angry with God for making me marry that man, but now I know that I really have no right to be talking to the creator of the world at all, let alone to be accusing him. And Hannah has always seemed so convinced that God is looking out for us, that I cannot help but think that he will do something to help me be happy still in all of this."

Athalia felt a terrible stab run through her body and she jumped to her feet. Fearing that she would blurt out her whole story if she were to remain in the girl's presence, she mumbled something about having to finish washing up and ran into the house, leaving a bewildered Rachel to stare at her.

∽

It was now or never.

The betrothal ceremony would take place in a matter of hours. Athalia had been invited to the feast that would follow at Rachel's house. This was quite an honor, as only family and a few close friends had been invited.

Athalia was familiar with the process. Elihu would be represented by a friend who would meet with Rachel's father and present him with Elihu's gifts, binding the contract. A feast would follow, and all would be settled. Rachel would be bound, by law, to Elihu.

To Elihu.

Her friend would be bound to the very man that sent chills down Athalia's spine, to the man that made her stomach turn violently, to the man who pretended devoted servitude to the God of Israel alone while making periodic visits to Baal's temple to have his own lusts satisfied.

Athalia's fists clenched tightly at her sides as repulsion pulsed its way through her small, but swelling, body.

"He's a good man, solid and upright . . ."

"Would never allow his daughter to marry anything less . . ."

Rachel's words echoed through Athalia's racing mind. She could feel the drops of perspiration forming on her forehead as her heart pounded. She alone had the means to stop it, to expose Elihu for who he really was.

Of course, this would mean that she, too, would be exposed. A prostitute. "A wicked, wretched sinner."

"Athalia?"

She turned gasping to see the concerned smile of Hannah.

"Are you all right?"

Athalia forced a smile and swiped at her damp forehead. "Yes, I am fine. Are you ready to go?"

∼

Hannah, Samuel, Athalia, and Micah all arrived together at Rachel's house. They were a bit early to help with the last-minute preparations, for, as Miriam had pointed out, "the drought left few with enough servants to set up properly for such an event."

Micah and Samuel left the women to help with the food while they went to help set up the tables. The feast would be held out of doors, and as Rachel's family was the richest in the village, it was quite a feast. Sheep were roasted, fruit and nuts were set in baskets all around, and the very best wine was presented. They were one of the few families that had tables at which to dine, and it was these the men were heaving out of the large house.

Micah picked up one end of a large cedar table and heaved. He and Samuel together lugged it to its appointed spot and set it down.

But not before Micah had turned suddenly towards the sound of cascading laughter.

The heavy cedar leg landed on his toe.

"Augh!"

Samuel quickly dropped his own end and ran to the aid of the now dancing Micah.

Try as he might, Samuel could not hold back the laughter at the sight of Micah dancing around on one foot. His laughter faded into a concerned sigh as he noted the direction to which Micah kept glancing. "You'd do better to keep your eyes on the inanimate objects. Remember, she is being betrothed to another."

Micah sighed and sat down to examine his now slightly swollen toe through his sandal.

"Well, if you think you might survive, I will leave you to your toe and help get the other tables."

Micah smiled, "Go ahead, I'm fine."

Micah could feel the blood pulsing through the injured toe as he wiggled it. Then he heard it again. He looked up to see the inadvertent cause of his injury. Rachel was standing with Hannah and Athalia, laughing. Herself the honored guest, she was humbly helping to prepare and set out the food for the feast. Her head was tossed back, and she was laughing as though this event was to fulfill her deepest desire. But Micah knew differently.

He knew she was struggling with this change in her own plans for her life, and yet, still, she laughed.

Micah looked up into the cloudless sky. "Oh, God, let him be good to her. Let him cherish her. Let her be happy."

Then, with one more glance toward Rachel, he picked himself up and limped back to help with another table.

～

Athalia's heart was thumping heavily as she placed the last of the food out on the tables. Everything was almost set.

"There he is!" Hannah whispered pointing to a well-dressed older man approaching on a camel leading a caravan of sheep and goats behind him. "That's Elihu's friend with the betrothal gifts for Rachel's father. Wow. That's more than the number of sheep we own all together!"

Athalia's heart gave a leap and she swallowed hard, trying not to stare after the man as he dismounted and strode towards the house where Rachel's father awaited.

This was it. If she was going to do it, it had to be now.

Slowly she dropped the basket of bread onto the table and, with a deep breath, turned and began to follow the man to the house. The sights around her melted into a dark haze as her eyes focused on the door ahead. She lifted one foot, then the other, forcing them forward.

From somewhere behind her she heard the faint voice of Hannah questioning her, but she did not turn, willing herself forward to what she must do. She was almost there. The door was within reach . . .

A sharp tug at her arm forced her to stop.

"Athalia! You cannot go in there! That's where the contract is being formed!"

Athalia turned, desperation in her eyes as she faced Hannah. "But you don't understand. I must. It is most important." She pulled herself violently away from Hannah's hold and flung herself at the door, running in, with Hannah close at her heels pleading with her to stop.

Two men whose heads had been bent over a scroll looked up, surprised by the sudden interruption. Before they could react, Athalia had dropped to her knees before them and had fallen on her face crying, "Please sirs, forgive your humble servant for the intrusion."

The older man, Rachel's father, looked up at Hannah who was now standing in the doorway, mouth dropped open in utter confusion.

"What is the meaning of this?"

Hannah shook her head helplessly. "I am sorry sir, I tried to stop her."

"It is extremely important that I tell you something before this continues, sir. You can throw me out after, but please hear what I have to say." Athalia lifted her face to the men, pleading.

With an exasperated wave of his arm, the man standing next to Rachel's father cried, "Who does this girl think she is, barging in like this? Throw her out, I say, and let's get on with it!"

Slowly Rachel's father turned to the man, eyes steady and piercing. "You say? This is my house, and I say who leaves and who stays. Is that clear?"

Then, turning back to the girl at his feet, he urged her, "You have won my curiosity. Now speak, child."

Athalia smiled gratefully and, taking a deep breath, began. "You see, sir, Elihu is not who you think he is, and nor am I. I am a runaway prostitute from the temple of Baal, a temple Elihu frequented regularly to, ah, pay his respects." At these words, she dropped her head in embarrassment.

Rachel's father dropped silently down onto a bench beside the table. His fists opened and closed in anger as he pondered the full implications.

After a moment, he lifted his face to Athalia again. "So, you can be certain that is was the same man, Elihu, that you saw in the temple?"

Athalia bowed her head. "I am certain. I did not merely see him there . . ." She broke off, ashamed. "He came to threaten me the other day when he recognized me at Samuel and Hannah's wedding feast."

The man's eyes grew dark with anger.

"Is this true?" he demanded of Hannah who was still, herself, trying to absorb all that was being revealed.

Hannah dropped her own gaze respectfully. "Sir, until just this moment I knew none of this, but I do know that someone saw a man threaten this girl in the woods during my own wedding feast."

For a moment all was silent.

Then Rachel's father rose and stood before the other man. "You may tell your friend that the whole thing is off. I will not have such a husband for my daughter. I know that much of Israel has changed with our present royal family, worshipping whomever and whatever they like, but I will not have it in this family. There is only one God of this house and he does not approve of such behavior. Now get out."

The words were spoken quietly, but there was no doubt about the conviction behind them.

"But sir, this girl, how can you possibly believe . . ." The man was pleading now, practically whining as he tried to change his mind.

"I said get out."

The look on Rachel's father's face made it quite clear that there would be no negotiating this decision, and the younger man exited quickly, grabbing the bag of jewels he had brought in with him, and glaring at the still prostrate girl on the floor.

For just a moment, all was silent in the room with Athalia still on her knees, Hannah, unable to move from shock, and Rachel's father pacing the floor, head in hand.

It was Athalia who finally broke the silence. "I am sorry sir, for this, and that I did not tell all sooner. I will inconvenience you no more." With that, she rose quickly from the floor and ran out the door.

"Athalia!" Hannah cried running to the door after her.

"No, please, Hannah, wait," Rachel's father called after her, "I need to know! Was there truly a witness to the threats? I would hate to think I've wrongly accused a man of such a vile act."

Hannah stopped and turned back for a moment. Rachel's father was rubbing his forehead and his voice was low and sad. Pity filled her heart for the man. "Yes, sir. A friend came to me after he saw a man threaten her, but the reasoning for the threat was unknown to him. He told me out of concern for the girl, and now I see there was much reason for concern. Please, sir, I must go after her."

"Yes, go. And thank you Hannah," the man said waving his arm. Then he slowly lowered himself back onto the bench, placing his head in his hands as Hannah left the room.

~

Micah tripped over a bench as the small form came rushing past him. He caught the quiet "I'm sorry" from the flying form that was halfway down the street by the time he sat down to rub his bruised shin. "Athalia?"

"So, I see you are rather accident-prone today, eh?"

Micah glanced up to see Samuel standing over him, laughing, once again, at his expense.

Micah pressed his lips together in a tight smile acknowledging the tease. "I think that was Athalia that flew past. I wonder where she is going in such a hurry?"

Samuel shrugged. "Maybe she forgot something from the house."

"Samuel! Micah! Have you seen Athalia?" a voice yelled from behind them.

Samuel and Micah exchanged glances as the panting Hannah came running up.

"She ran past a few moments ago." Micah put a hand to his eyes to deflect the sun and nodded down the road. "Yes, I can still see her. Why? What's wrong?"

"I will explain later. I've got to catch up to her."

Hannah picked up the hem of her tunic and took off in the direction Micah had indicated.

"But Hannah! The feast!"

Hannah turned her head, still running and yelled, "I don't think there's going to be a feast!"

Samuel put his hands on his hips and shook his head at his new wife running down the village street.

Micah, on the other hand, was focused only on the strange words she had uttered. No feast? What could that mean? Was Rachel not to be betrothed?

~

"Athalia! Stop! Please!"

The girl's pace had slowed a bit, allowing Hannah to catch up.

Too tired to outrun her pursuer, Athalia fell, sobbing, to the side of the dirt road just outside the village.

Hannah, exhausted herself, stood panting over the girl with her hands on her knees trying to catch her breath.

The next few moments were spent in silence, broken only by the sobs of the distraught girl.

"I am sorry I lied." Athalia's eyes, red and swollen, remained fixed on the dusty road beneath her. "I was just going to wait until the baby was born and then leave. I know I don't have the right to stay with you, but I thought maybe you would raise my baby to serve your God." A tear fell to the dust. "Maybe your God would show him mercy anyway. He hasn't done anything wrong."

"So, this is what you are doing now? Leaving?" Hannah spoke quietly and sat down beside the girl.

Athalia's head flew up, eyes opened wide. "Well, I can't stay with you. You are godly people. I am a prostitute."

Hannah placed her hands behind her head and leaned back to look up at the clear sky.

"Have you heard of King David?"

Athalia cocked her head at the odd question. "Wasn't he the most famous king of Israel?"

Hannah nodded. "Yes. God promised him that a descendant of his would always reign on the throne of Israel."

"I do remember hearing that somewhere, but what . . . ?" Athalia was thoroughly confused.

Hannah pulled her knees up to her chest and began. "Back when the Israelites were still wandering around in the desert after God had brought them out of Egypt, the leader, Joshua, sent some men into Jericho to spy out the land. They went to a harlot's house to stay."

Athalia's eyes grew wide at the mention of a harlot.

Hannah continued, "While they were there, she hid them from the men of the city who had found out about them. Because she risked her own life to save these men, they promised her that if, when they came back to destroy the city, she hung a scarlet cord from her window, she and her household would be saved. Well, when they came back with the whole army of Israel, God had them march around the city for seven days, and then God made the walls of the city collapse."

Hannah turned to look into Athalia's tear stained face. "All except one small section of wall which remained standing. It was the house of the prostitute."

Athalia turned to meet Hannah's gaze. She swallowed hard.

"The prostitute's name was Rahab," Hannah continued, "and she lived with the Israelites the rest of her life. She married and became the great, great grandmother of King David."

They sat in silence for a moment.

"Is that story true?" Athalia finally whispered.

Hannah nodded.

"So, you think your God would show mercy to me? I don't even think I am a Hebrew."

"I believe God shows mercy to anyone who fears him."

Athalia's eyes dropped back to the dirt. "I just don't know how . . ."

Hannah laid a gentle hand on Athalia's shoulder. "I would really like for you to stay with us, for your sake and the baby's."

Athalia looked up into the sincere eyes of her new friend. She knew that Hannah meant what she said. But what about the others? The news was sure to spread quickly through the village.

As though reading her mind, Hannah added, "And don't worry about what other's will think. Many of the villagers frequent the temple of Baal themselves. They are just as much a part of that as you were. As a matter of fact, I am surprised that no one else has recognized you." Then she laughed. "Of course, to be admitting that would be admitting visits to the temple, wouldn't it?"

Slowly Hannah rose to her feet and held out her hand. "Come on. Let's go home."

Athalia lifted her eyes. Where else did she have to go? Slowly, she reached out and took the outstretched hand.

10

ATHALIA STOOD WATCHING THE flock happily grazing on the patches
of green that had sprung from the earth in the weeks following the
big rains. After finding out that her flute had likely belonged once to
a shepherd, her curiosity had been stirred, and Athalia had begun a
habit of coming out to the pastures behind the village to watch the
sheep when there was a break from the daily chores.

She observed as Micah kept watch, intrigued by the way he
interacted with the sheep, and the sheep with him. Micah appeared always on alert. The sheep appeared never on alert. As
Micah's watchful eye scanned the flock often, Athalia noticed that
the sheep seemed unaware of his presence most of the time, preoc-
cupied with feeding their bellies.

And they appeared often in need of rescue. She had seen
Micah take the wooden stopper out of the ram's horn he carried
around his waist and pour oil on the wounds of a sheep who had
managed to get itself stuck in a bramble bush. She had seen him
use his staff to pull wandering sheep back into the herd, and once
saw him use his rod to scare off a young wolf. Yet, through all of

this, the flock seemed aware of neither danger nor the one protecting them.

They seemed unaware, that is, until Micah called to them. That was a sight to see, when he called, and every sheep slowly lifted its head and lumbered towards the caller.

On this particular afternoon, Micah had seen her coming and asked if she would mind watching the flock for a bit so that he could take care of something. Athalia had agreed, smiling as she noticed that he had walked off in the direction of the field that Rachel's father owned.

As she observed the feeding sheep, Athalia hoped that none would wander off in his absence, not yet fully confident in her ability to wield the rod or staff he had left with her. But all appeared well for the moment. The sheep seemed content to stay close. And there, just outside the circle of its grazing family, lay the peaceful lamb. She smiled as the wooly creature stretched lazily and yawned, exposing the tiny pink tongue.

"He has to die, you know."

Athalia looked around to see a serious little face staring hard past her at the lamb. Nathaniel stood, hands on hips, shaking his head slowly. Despite the grim words that had been spoken, Athalia had to hide the smile that surfaced at the stoic demeanor of the child who had appeared so suddenly beside her.

"And it is all for us." Nathaniel sighed dramatically.

Turning to the boy, Athalia cocked her head slightly. "For us, you say?"

Nathaniel nodded slowly. "Daddy says it is for you too, now that you are part of the family and all. Even if you don't go with us to Jerusalem, Daddy is going to lay his hand on the lamb's head for you."

Athalia turned back to the lamb. She knew about sacrifices. At Baal's temple there were sacrifices daily. She guessed this was that to which the child was referring.

"It doesn't seem fair, you know, that he has to die instead of us. It's not him who does the bad stuff. It's us," Nathaniel said, still staring at the lamb soberly.

"Die instead of us?" This confused Athalia. People sacrificed to Baal to get something from him, anything from good weather to just plain good fortune, but what was this boy talking about?

Nathaniel looked up at her quizzically. "Didn't your mom or dad tell you about it?"

Athalia shook her head.

"Daddy says we deserve to die because we do bad stuff, and God never does, but he lets us kill a lamb for him instead. And it has to be the best lamb we've got. So, the lamb gets punished 'stead of us."

Intrigued, Athalia nodded for the boy to continue.

"Daddy says it's because God loves us, so he figured out a way for us to be with him even though we all do bad stuff."

Athalia dropped her head. Bad stuff. Yes, she had done her share of bad stuff. "Some bad stuff is worse than others," she whispered quietly.

"Daddy says we all do bad stuff. He says it doesn't matter how bad we think it is. It's all the same to God. It's bad, and we all need something to die for it."

"But why would God do it that way? Why would he give us a way out when we don't deserve it?"

Nathaniel shook his head and threw up his arms in exasperation. "I told you! 'Cause he loves us! He wants to be with us!"

A single tear ran down Athalia's cheek. It did not go unnoticed by the boy.

"Yeah, I was sad too." Nathaniel turned to look at the lamb and shook his head slowly. "It doesn't seem fair that Shalom has to die, but it's the only way, Daddy says. That's the way God made it. At least we don't have to die."

"Shalom? Is that what you call the lamb?" Athalia smiled slightly as Nathaniel nodded.

"I got to name him."

Shalom. How interesting that the boy had chosen that name for the very lamb who would make peace between God and his family, the lamb who would make all well between God and man. Athalia turned to smile at the boy. The tears were flowing fast now.

"Look! Here he comes!"

The lamb, who had heard the voices, had risen to his feet and was making his way slowly over to them. Athalia watched as the boy ran forward to meet his doomed friend. They wrestled around for a while until the lamb grew tired of it and lay down. Athalia noticed then that the boy glanced her way for a moment with an odd look in his eye. Then he turned back to the sedate lamb and pulled something from his belt. What was he doing? His head was bent over the lamb now, so that Athalia could not see what was happening. Then he rose slowly and walked back toward Athalia. There was something clutched tightly in his hand.

"Here." Nathaniel held out his hand to Athalia, slowly opening it.

"What . . . ?" Athalia reached out to take the wad of white wool.

"It's so whenever you're sad about Shalom having to die, you can look at it and remember that it was for you, so you don't have to get punished. Then maybe you will feel better."

He pulled another piece of wool from his belt. "That's what I do."

Athalia looked down at the matted wool in her palm. Two tears dropped onto it. Slowly her gaze rose back to the intense face of the boy standing over her, clutching tightly to his own piece of the lamb.

"Thank you," she said quietly.

"You have a flute like Micah's."

The boy's sudden change of topics startled Athalia, and she laughed. "Yes, I was told it is a shepherd's flute."

Nathaniel shrugged. "I just know it is like one that Micah carries when he takes the sheep way out for the summer months. Did you quit being a shepherdess?"

Athalia looked down at the ground. "No, I was never a shepherdess."

"So, the flute was your father's?" Nathaniel continued to inquire, oblivious to the tense manner with which he was answered.

"I don't know," Athalia said looking down into the boy's face. Something about the matter-of-factness of the questioning gave her the boldness to face the answers. "I never knew my father. Or my mother."

Nathaniel's face wrinkled in confusion.

"I was left as a baby outside of a temple. The flute was left in the basket with me."

"And I wonder if it was a message to you," another voice cut in.

They turned to see Hannah approaching.

"I wonder if whoever left you at the temple door wanted you to know that you were loved. That you were their little lamb," Hannah said, joining the little group.

"I've often imagined it something like that," Athalia said with a sigh, "that it was out of love that they left me, that they were unable to care for me for some reason, but I just don't know."

"And you will never know for certain. But you can be certain that there is one who cares about you as a shepherd cares about his lambs."

"I'm guessing you mean your God?" Athalia said quizzically. "That seems a strange analogy."

"It wasn't strange for King David. You remember the king whose great, great grandmother was Rahab?"

Athalia nodded.

"Well long before he was king, he was a shepherd, and he wrote a song that compared God to a shepherd and himself to a sheep."

"Oh yeah!" Nathaniel piped in, "That's the song mama sings to us all the time!"

Then, taking a deep breath, Nathaniel began singing at the top of his lungs,

> "The LORD is my shepherd;
> I shall not want.
> He makes me to lie down in green pastures;
> He leads me beside the still waters.
> He restores my soul;
> He leads me in the paths of righteousness
> For His name's sake.

Yea, though I walk through the valley of the shadow of death,
I will fear no evil;
For You are with me;
Your rod and Your staff, they comfort me.

You prepare a table before me in the presence of my enemies;
You anoint my head with oil;
My cup runs over.
Surely goodness and mercy shall follow me
All the days of my life;
And I will dwell in the house of the LORD
Forever."[1]

Athalia smiled, recognizing some of the very things she had observed of Micah with his flock. "Can you teach me that song, Nathaniel?"

~

Athalia sat down with her back to the olive tree. She closed her eyes and drank deeply the peace of the morning. All was well. They knew, and still they accepted her. They treated her as though she had been born into the family. They continued to tell her that God accepted her as well. Every day as she experienced the compassion of the wonderful family, she grew more and more to believe it herself. Maybe God did forgive her. Maybe, like Rahab, he would have pity on her and her unborn child.

"What must Rahab have thought, sitting up in her own house as the walls of the city all around her began to crash down?" Athalia thought to herself. "Did she really believe that she would be saved? That the God of the Israelites would look down kindly on her after all she had done? Or was she scared? Did she wait fearfully as the rest of Jericho did, staring down at the army as day after day they just marched around, biding their time? And for what? How could they have known that in the end it would be an almighty hand from above that would crush them, without a single sword being raise against them? And at what point did Rahab truly know she had been forgiven?"

1. Psalm 23 (NKJV)

Then she laughed out loud. "It was probably," she thought, "the moment that she realized that hers was the only house left standing! That would have been some solid evidence!"

She smiled contentedly and raised the flute to her lips.

Suddenly the flute was ripped out of her hands. Before she had time to look up, she felt a sting as a rough hand came into hard contact with her cheek.

"So, the whore stuck around!"

Athalia could feel the hot breath on her own hands which now guarded her smarting face.

"What did you think? That I'd go slinking back to Shechem and leave things unsettled between us?"

Athalia shook, hands still tightly guarding her face, afraid even to open her eyes.

"Or did you think Baal might come to save you?"

Athalia felt her heart racing as fear crept over her. "O God," she mouthed silently behind her hands, "please show me mercy!"

Suddenly, with a strength she did not know she had, Athalia lowered her hands and stared calmly into the evil eyes that were inches away from her own. She opened her mouth, and no one was more surprised than she when the following words came out: "I serve the one true God now, the one who brought fire down from heaven and caused it to lick up even the water."

Elihu drew back, caught off guard by the sudden boldness of the statement. Quickly regaining his composure, he glared back. "What makes you think that God wants anything to do with the likes of you? There is nothing you could possibly do to make up for your life of harlotry!"

"That's why it's called mercy." As the words left Athalia's mouth, she suddenly believed them. That was it. Mercy. She now served a merciful God. Who in this world could possibly deserve to be loved by a holy, all powerful God? If there was no mercy, then all were doomed. But the evidence was pointing continually to the fact that he did, indeed, care for his people. Therefore, he must be a God of mercy. And she was a grateful recipient of that mercy. She reached to feel the soft wad of wool tucked into the belt around her waist.

Elihu's eyes burned with anger. "Well, for ruining my life, you will receive no mercy."

He reached out and grabbed her braid, pulling her head tightly back to look full into his face. His lips twisted into a deformed smile. "You are a pretty little thing. Pity. Such a waste."

Surprisingly to herself, the terror had melted away from Athalia, so that now she sat calmly waiting for Elihu's intentions to become known. It was soon becoming apparent, for she felt the pressure as his hands wrapped tightly around her small neck and squeezed. She tried to scream, but the grip was too tight. She could get no breath. She was amazed at how clear her thoughts were at this moment. Though she hurt tremendously, all that Athalia could think about was the mercy of God and how she really hoped that it was true; for she suspected that she would soon find out.

"Yea though I walk thru the valley of the shadow of death, I will fear no evil for You are with me . . ."[2] The words passed softly through her brain as she felt the life run out of her.

Then, just as the world faded from her view, she heard a thud, and she felt the grip release. She fell to the ground as the breath rushed painfully in to fill her lungs.

"Are you all right?"

The question sounded so far away. The world was still spinning as Athalia looked up and tried to focus, still gasping for air, her hands tightly guarding her throat. A blurry face . . . a gentle hand on her shoulder . . . then everything went black.

～

"What will happen to him?"

Hannah looked into the troubled eyes. "David is safe. He is on his way to a city of refuge where no one from Elihu's family can avenge his blood for now. Micah went with him. If someone comes forward to claim vengeance, then there will be a trial at the city gate."

2. Psalm 23:4a (NKJV)

Athalia looked down at her wringing hands. "How did he find me?"

Hannah smiled. "Apparently he has become familiar with your habit of going off to that olive grove to play your flute. He said he would often check to see if you were there."

Athalia blushed.

"He did not want to make you feel uncomfortable," Hannah continued, "so he would just listen from a distance, he said. But today, when the music stopped abruptly, he became concerned and . . . well, you know what happened."

As she spoke the words aloud, Hannah was suddenly aware of the irony of David's plight. He had said that when he had realized the severity of the situation, he had picked up a rock and hit Elihu in the back of the head, just like he had done to Samuel a few weeks ago.

Hannah closed her eyes as she considered how David must be feeling right now. It was not long ago that she had voiced her desire that he feel the fear and hurt that she had felt when Samuel was missing. It was likely that her wish was being granted.

Then her eyes flew opened as she realized with surprise, that she no longer wanted that for him; Hannah genuinely wanted him to be free from accusation. "I've finally forgiven him!" she thought to herself with a smile. Apparently, the habit she had formed of saying aloud, "I forgive him" every time the painful memory had surfaced had proved fruitful. Apparently, the words had finally sunk deep enough to drown the bitterness.

Athalia moaned, drawing Hannah's attention back to the present situation. "I have caused so much trouble."

"Well I know at least one person who would argue with that," Hannah said with a laugh as a form came flying across the field towards them.

"Athalia! Are you badly hurt? How awful that must have been!" Rachel pushed the wild strands of hair back from her face as she flopped down beside her new friend and grabbed hold of the still wringing hands. "Oh! The bruises on your neck!"

Athalia looked up with a weak smile. "I'm fine. It's nothing, really. It's David I am worried about."

"Oh, don't trouble yourself about that! Daddy thinks he is a hero. When his wife started getting worked up about the whole thing, he told her in no uncertain terms that she was to hold her tongue. He said that he would defend David if it came to trial, but he is doubtful anyone would come forward to seek vengeance as Elihu had very little family other than Daddy's wife, and, like I said, Daddy has taken care of that."

Athalia looked gratefully into the flushed face of the kind girl. She smiled. "I am so glad you are not going to have to marry that awful man."

Rachel's eyes misted and she put her hand on Athalia's shoulder. "And I am so glad you never have to worry about him again."

"All is well," Hannah whispered as she watched the two girls embrace.

11

"Worthy is the Lamb who was slain to receive power and riches and wisdom, and strength and honor and glory and blessing!"

REVELATION 5:12 (NKJV)

NATHANIEL SAT SILENTLY WATCHING his tiny sister laugh and play on the mat. Jerusha would be right back, she had said. This, he knew, was a big responsibility; it was an opportunity to show how grown up he was.

But he did not really want it. Being with Abbigail just made him miss Mama more. How could she just play and laugh when her Mama, and his, was gone?

What he really wanted was to talk to Shalom.

A tear trickled quietly down his cheek.

Shalom had been the perfect listener, never interrupting as he poured out his heart, never distracted or too busy, never telling him how he should be feeling or acting.

Now his heart was so full of things that needed to be said . . . that needed to be heard . . . that Nathaniel thought he might burst. It hurt to hold it in.

He glanced over at the tiny child wriggling around on her back, little legs pumping, little fists boxing the air.

"It is not her fault, Nathaniel," Mama had told him, "and now she will need her big brother more than ever."

"Do you even know she is dead?" he whispered. As though sensing the weight of the question, the baby's legs stopped kicking and the big brown eyes stared up into the sad eyes of the boy.

"Did you even know that when all those people came, and we wrapped Mama up and took her away on that flat board that she was never going to come back again?"

Nathaniel swiped away a tear and looked off into the distance. "Daddy said that the board is called a bier and it was so we could carry her to the tomb. That's where her body will stay from now on. She's never coming home again."

The baby lay very still.

"Did you know that those seven days we stayed in the house were for mourning?" Nathaniel continued, "Daddy said that just means that it was time for us to be sad because she is gone. That was three weeks ago. But I'm still sad. I don't think seven days was enough to get all the sad out."

For a moment there was silence as Nathaniel absently caressed the tiny, chubby arm of his sister.

Suddenly the baby grabbed Nathaniel's finger. Startled, Nathaniel jumped slightly and looked down into the big brown eyes that were still fixed on his tearstained face. A slight smile flashed briefly across his countenance before fading again into the shadow of grief.

"Everything is changing, Abbigail," Nathaniel continued with a sigh, "first Mama, and now Shalom . . ." His voice trailed off.

"He's being prepared, you know," he said slowly, quietly, looking intently into the wide eyes of the captivated infant. "Shalom, I mean. That's why we are here."

Nathaniel swallowed hard. Very seriously he added, "The lamb must die, you know Abbigail, for us, he must die."

The tears were flowing freely now as the boy let loose the flood of hurting and confused thoughts that had been piling up during the two-day trip to Jerusalem.

"That's why we are here," he repeated slowly.

After a moment, Nathaniel wiped his eyes and got down on his stomach right beside the baby, propping his chin up with his elbows.

"But not all the changes are sad, you know," he said reaching out to pat the soft tuft of hair on the little head. "Rachel will be moving in. It won't be for another year though. Micah asked her dad if he could marry her, so they are betrothed now. That means he can't see her for a whole year! Micah doesn't seem sad about it though. He smiles all the time, and I heard him humming last week while he was building the extra room onto our house. That's where he and Rachel will stay.

"And we got to come on this trip. Daddy says it's beautiful. The temple I mean. I don't remember it. I was too little last time I came."

Abbigail laughed and poked a chubby finger at Nathaniel's nose.

Nathaniel smiled. And this time the smile stayed put.

∼

"There it is!" Nathaniel grabbed hold of Abbigail with one hand and pointed excitedly with the other, "It's Solomon's temple! It's so big! Look how little the people look that are going in and out of it!"

Jerusha, who was holding the baby, smiled at the child's enthusiasm, glad to see that he had finally begun to take an interest in his little sister.

The baby giggled and strained down to reach her boisterous brother.

"Look! Those are the priests! One of them will go into the holy of holies . . ." Suddenly his eyes dropped and misted, "That's where they will take Shalom."

Jerusha laid a gentle hand on the boy's shoulder.

As they drew closer, Nathaniel's eyes grew wide with the splendor of the structure. His neck strained back to see the towering arches of the pillars high above. "Daddy says it is forty-five feet tall, Abbigail. Forty-five feet! There is nothing in our village that tall!"

He took a deep breath, inhaling the sweet scent of the cedar. "Can you smell that Abbigail? That is cedar that covers every bit of the inside of the temple! You can't even see a bit of the stone through it! Daddy said that every single stone was carved individually to fit each of the others. But they carved them at a stone quarry far away from the temple so no sound of any iron tools could be heard inside the temple."

Their pace slowed as they stepped onto the pillared porch which welcomed the pilgrims to the temple. The huge wooden doors stood wide open.

"Look at all the flowers and palm trees, Abbigail," Nathaniel said, pointing to the detailed carvings on the doors covered in gold that glistened in the morning sun.

"Nathaniel."

The boy looked up as his father approached. And there trotting along beside him was his beloved Shalom. The splendor of the temple faded from his eyes as Nathaniel remembered the sole purpose of their visit on this particular morning.

Joseph bent down on one knee in front of Nathaniel. "I thought you might like to say good-bye," he said, his eyes reflecting the pain that he knew his dear son was experiencing.

Nathaniel dropped to his knees beside the fluffy lamb on the rope by which his father had led him. He buried his face in the soft wool and cried silently. After a moment, he released himself from the lamb and looked into the big, innocent eyes. "Thank you," he whispered softly.

Then, with the composure of one much older, Nathaniel arose solemnly and, looking straight ahead towards the temple doors, took Jerusha's hand as his father led his precious lamb off to the slaughter.